HALO MOON

Sharon Cohen

Quercus

QUERCUS CHILDREN'S BOOKS

First published in Great Britain in 2019 by Hodder and Stoughton

1 3 5 7 9 10 8 6 4 2

A CIP catalogue record for this book
is available from the British Library.

ISBN 978 1 786 54010 2

Typeset in Avenir and Sabon by Avon DataSet Ltd,
Bidford-on-Avon, Warwickshire

Printed and bound in Great Britain by CPI Group (UK) Ltd,
Croydon, CR0 4YY

The paper and board used in this book
are made from wood from responsible sources.

MIX
Paper from
responsible sources
FSC® C104740

Quercus Children's Books
An imprint of Hachette Children's Group
Part of Hodder and Stoughton
Carmelite House
50 Victoria Embankment
London EC4Y 0DZ

An Hachette UK Company
www.hachette.co.uk

www.hachettechildrens.co.uk

To Mary
who used to sing 'The Happy Wanderer'
on beautiful walks in the Lake District.

'Remember to look up at the stars.'
Stephen Hawking (1942–2018)

PREFACE

There's a hundred ways to start this story, a hundred ways to tell it. Each one is impossible. Each one, unbelievable. But it did all happen and I promise it's all true.

There was a boy with eyelashes the shape of crescent moons and a star-gazing girl with burning amber hair and a dark-skinned stranger from a faraway land who told us this: there is a time, there is a place, there is a moment when it will happen, and there is nothing we can do to stop it.

So I'll just go on and tell the tale. As it was. As it is. As if it's happening right now and I'm living it again and you're living the story through me.

TEN ...

1

Halo

My name is Halo Moon, at least that's what they call me, those who've known me since I was born. It was the first word I said when Gran lifted me to the window one bright shining night.

'Look at that moon, Halo, just look at that beautiful moon.'

I stopped grizzling and looked.

'Moo,' I said, pointing. 'Moo.'

Mum says I was born with my head tilted upwards.

I got my first telescope on my seventh birthday. I'm twelve now.

'You're on the cusp, my girl,' Gran says.

When I ask her what she means she just winks and smiles.

It all starts in July when the new boy arrives. His bedroom is diagonally opposite mine and I keep peeping around the curtains to see if he's there.

It's Monday evening, about nine thirty. I'm in the front garden now, in my sky watcher's chair waiting for it to go dark. I look up and the new boy is standing in the road, peering over our hedge.

'What are you looking at?' he says.

'I'm waiting for the meteors,' I say, 'but it's not dark enough yet.'

He's taller than I thought and his eyes are different colours.

'Can I come round?' he says.

'Yeah, if you like.'

His shirt collar's turned up and he's wearing white canvas shoes.

'My name is Pedro. Pedro Ortega.' He holds out his right hand.

For a moment, I don't know what to do. I've never shaken hands with anyone before. I get up from my chair.

'Halo Moon,' I say.

'Very pleased to meet you, Halo Moon.'

His hand is warm and soft. I sit down again feeling like I should say something. Pedro sits next to me on the grass.

'How old are you?' he says.

'How old d'you think?'

He shrugs. 'Same age as me. Twelve?'

I smile and nod.

'Have you lived here long?' he says.

'I was born here.' I look at his floppy fringe and curling eyelashes. 'What brought you here?' I ask.

He stares at the ground and there's a sort of sadness in his eyes. 'My mum got a new job.'

'What does she do?'

'She works in a bank. International section. She has to travel quite a bit.'

'What about your dad?'

He looks down like he doesn't want to say.

The sky's starting to turn. That deep, deep blue before night comes.

'We'll be able to see the Perseids in August,' I say. 'All the burning dust and ice from the comet Swift-Tuttle. Astronomers used to think it was going to crash into Earth but they don't think that any more.'

Pedro scowls and gazes at the sky. 'No need

to worry about that then,' he says. 'Is that your room?' He points to my dormer window.

'Yeah.'

'Thought so. Can I come back later and look through your telescope?'

I'm surprised how confident he is. I pause. I'm not sure. But his smile is wide and lovely and I can't help smiling back.

He bounces to his feet. 'See you later then, Halo Moon.' And he disappears around the hedge.

I go inside to get a snack. Mum's seeing to Gran. She's had a little 'accident' and needs a clean-up and a shower.

Dad's at the table supping beer. 'That the new lad?'

'His name's Pedro.'

'Talks nicely.'

'You weren't listening, were you?'

Dad smiles. 'Not on purpose.'

I make toast and sprinkle it with cinnamon.

'Am I all right being out after midnight? Pedro's coming back to look at the stars.'

Dad gives me a wink.

'Oh, stop it,' I say.

'Yeah, 'course it's all right,' says Dad. 'Lock the door when you come in and let me know you're safe inside if I've fallen asleep.'

It's just past eleven. I'm back in my sky watcher's chair. It has a padded seat and leans backwards. There's a flask of hot tea by my side and a bag of dates.

The sky is huge and sparkling and the air is cooling. Pedro turns up in a matching T-shirt and baseball cap. He spreads a blanket over the grass.

'If we're lucky we might see the Delta Aquarids,' I say.

'Stars?' says Pedro.

'Meteors, actually. Best after midnight, though.' I glance at him. 'Want to look at Mars?'

''Course,' he says.

I let him sit in my chair. He leans forward and looks into the eyepiece.

'Turn this to focus,' I say.

He screws up one eye. He's smiling already, then he lets out a gasp. 'Awesome!' he says. He looks again. 'It's so bright and orange and beautiful!'

He's grinning like crazy.

'That is . . . *the* coolest thing . . . Halo Moon.' And he nestles in the chair again and stares and stares.

It's not long before he jumps up and starts jigging around. He rubs his arms and legs then glances at his phone. 'Eleven-thirty,' he says. 'I'm going to run up the hill.' He's got a mad look on his face and his eyes are twinkling.

'What for?'

'To warm up.' He sets off over the garden.

I glance at the telescope. You can't see it from the road and I'm sure no one's going to pinch it, but I drape the blanket over just in case.

'Wait. I'm coming with you,' I say.

We're standing in the middle of Halley Road grinning at each other. It seems like madness but there are no cars. Pedro charges and I follow. Full pelt. Usain-flipping-Bolt. Past the Fitchetts and the Thackreys and the Howeths with their garden gnomes. Past Doctor Shah's on Heatherlands Nook and the Prestons and the Ackroyds. I grit my teeth as the road gets steeper. I'm even closing on Pedro as we reach the top. We crash into the wall by the churchyard. Our chests are heaving and we slump in the gloom by the gravestones to catch our breath.

'Completely crackers,' I say.

Pedro leans over and pants. 'Feeling a bit warmer now,' he says.

A car passes. Its lights streak over us and we press ourselves to the wall like fugitives on the run. We glance at each other and grin. Then we giggle. Then we catch the laughing bug that makes your eyes stream and your ribs ache and you can't stand up any more. Minutes later we're sitting by the road trying not to look at each other. We're bunching our lips together to stop the giggles seeping out.

'What if we can't stop?' I say. 'What if laughing's like an incurable virus?'

Pedro has both hands locked over his mouth but his eyes give him away. Laughter bursts out again and we're rolling on the ground in fits of giggles.

A man walks past with his dog and we calm down a bit and take deep breaths.

'Where were you before you came here?' I say.

Pedro fills his lungs and blows out slowly like it's going to be a long story.

'An international school in Switzerland. My sister was there, too. She's sort of always been there to look after me.' He shrugs. 'But we've lived all over.'

'All over the world?'

'Yeah, wherever Mum or Dad's job has been. We were in the US before Switzerland, and Singapore before that.'

The world suddenly bursts open in my head. It expands beyond this village, beyond Yorkshire, beyond London, to places on the other side of the globe.

'And you've ended up here?' I say. 'In the middle of flipping nowhere?'

Pedro shrugs. 'It's been all right, so far,' he says.

It's nearly midnight. Meteor time. We get up and stride back down the hill. I leave Pedro in the garden and creep into the kitchen to get him a cup so he can have some tea. Dad pops his head around the door.

'How many?' he whispers.

'Haven't seen any yet.'

'Hungry?' he says.

'A bit.' I grab a couple of apples and my NASA mug and dash outside again.

Pedro's flat-out on the blanket. I settle down next to him and show him how to find the constellation Aquarius. We fix our eyes on that part of the sky.

'Keep watching,' I say. 'And don't blink, not even once.'

The night is still. Just the faint rumble of a car somewhere. We hold our breath.

'There!' I point.

A brilliant white dust trail hurtles above.

'Yes!' says Pedro.

More meteors streak like silver rips in the blackness. We squeal every time. I glance at him. See the brightness in his eyes.

'Makes you think, doesn't it?' I say.

'What does it make you think, Halo Moon?'

'How small we are. How piddlingly insignificant we are compared to all of that.'

Another one streaks away. And another. Pedro's clapping now. He's stamping his feet. Punching the air. He shakes a fist at the sky.

'Come on! You're showing off!' he shouts.

We're making far too much noise but we don't care. Those fireballs, those burning pieces of ancient space rock are the same age as our solar system – four and a half *billion* years old. If you can't shout about that, you can't shout about anything.

It's nearly one in the morning. We've counted seventeen. We've gobbled the apples and slurped the last of our tea.

His phone beeps and we see his sister at the window.

'I should be getting back,' he says. He does a funny bow then puts on a posh voice. 'I thank you, Halo Moon, for a night never to be forgotten. I will see you tomorrow.' And he turns and strides away across the road.

The sound of 'tomorrow' lingers in the cool air. I take everything inside and lock the door. I whisper to Dad that I'm back, then race upstairs to peep through the curtains. I don't know what I'm expecting. Maybe he'll wave.

Minutes pass. I see his light go on, then off again.

Then nothing.

2

Ageze

Grandma is worried about Father Abraham. There was a fierce storm in the night. Lightning ripped open the sky and the rain fell so hard it stung my face. Father Abraham's church is on top of a hill, the highest point for miles around.

'Ageze, go and check on him,' says Grandma. 'He may be closer to God up there, but he is also closer to the storm.'

Every year, I visit Grandma for one week during the school holiday. She lives in a small village in the north of Ethiopia. The rest of the time I live with my mother, father and two younger sisters in Addis Ababa, the capital city, where I was born. Da, Dr Hailu Tadesse, is an engineer in charge of building a wind farm. His favourite phrase is, 'We must cut carbon.' He even sings it in the shower. Ma, Sophia Tadesse, is a teacher.

I set off from Grandma's house to walk up the

steep slope to the church. The rain has loosened rocks and carved deep gullies in the ground. My feet sink into the soft earth. As I climb, the sun begins to spread its long fingers over the hill and, in the distance, I see something glinting.

Is it a coin? A gun? The sword of an ancient warrior?

I fix my eye on the bright point of light and move quickly across the slope.

As I peer at the ground, all I can see is a curved rim. It is a dull golden colour with lines around the edge. I scrape away the damp earth then use a stick to ease out the deeper, drier soil. Bit by bit, I break up the hard lumps and pile them on one side.

Through the quiet morning air, I hear the priests chanting, reminding me that I must check on Father Abraham.

Go quickly, I tell myself. *It will not take long.*

I am on my feet, about to race up the hill, when I hear voices. A group of villagers are on their way to church. If they see me, they will ask what I am doing. I grab fallen branches and pile them over the golden object, then clamber out of sight. With my eyes tightly shut, I hear their chattering voices moving closer.

I keep perfectly still, listening to the swish of their clothes and the tap, tap, tap of their sandals. If they find me, I will say that I am here to watch the sun rise. They seem to be moving away now, taking an easier route between the rocks and boulders. I must work fast in case someone else comes. I scrape away the earth, lump by lump, piece by piece, crumb by crumb. Checking on Father Abraham will have to wait.

Each swipe of the soil reveals more of the golden disc. How long has it been buried here and who did it belong to? I dig deeper until I can grasp both sides. I gently ease it out of the ground and rub it clean.

It is about twenty centimetres wide and round the edge and between each line, there is a strange script etched onto the surface. My fingers tremble as I touch the shapes carved so delicately into the metal.

It is truly the most beautiful and mysterious object I have ever seen.

As well as lines and writing, there is a hole at the centre, scratched and worn, as if the disc was once attached to something.

More villagers are making their way up the hill. I must move fast. I cannot show the disc to Father

Abraham. I am sure he would take it away from me and lock it in the storehouse next to the church.

As I get to my feet, something else catches my eye. I reach down and pull it from the soil. It is a small strip of dark metal with a hole at one end and a point at the other – like the hand of a clock. I fit the pointer over the hole in the disc. It seems to be the right size. But if it is meant to be a pointer, it is much too short to reach the edge. I think for a moment. Surely this can only mean one thing? There must be a longer pointer and another, smaller disc still buried in the ground.

The priests are chanting and singing again.

I am coming, Father Abraham. I am on my way!

I use branches and leaves to cover the disc once more, then race as fast as I can up the hill.

Father Abraham is a tiny man with a yellow hat and a grey whiskery beard. The villagers are gathered around him talking about the tiles that tumbled from the roof during the storm. I greet him and ask if I can help.

'If we all work together,' he says, 'the church will be restored in no time. We will start tomorrow.'

I know it is wrong of me but I wonder how much

time I will have to search for the missing pointer and the missing disc if I am helping to mend the church roof.

Later, I go back to the hiding place and carefully remove the pile of branches and leaves, then wrap the disc and pointer in my T-shirt and walk back to Grandma's house, where I hide them in my bag.

Grandma is anxious to know about Father Abraham.

'There is no need to worry,' I tell her. 'Father Abraham is very well. The rain washed some tiles from the roof but that is all. I will go back tomorrow to help to repair it.'

Grandma smiles and cooks me eggs for breakfast.

The next day I wake with the sun. There is a breeze as I climb the hill. The church is the colour of the Caribbean Sea. It can be seen from miles away. The villagers arrive with a handmade ladder and it is my job to hold it steady. Father Abraham stands nearby and watches. He is too old to climb ladders or carry roof tiles.

'Did I tell you that underneath this great hill is another church?' he says.

He has told this story many times but I still love to hear it.

'When we dug the foundations, buried beneath was a temple. In ancient times, the temple came under attack and to defend itself it sank below the ground.'

Father Abraham studies me.

'Do I see disbelief in your eyes, young man?'

'I am sorry, Father Abraham, but it is difficult to believe that a temple can disappear by itself.'

There is a twinkle in his eyes. He asks another worker to take my place and hold the ladder. 'I am happy that you have come to help with the church roof,' he says, 'so in reward, I have something to show you. Come with me.'

This is the first time I have been allowed in the back of the church. I have always wanted to see inside, but until now, Father Abraham has kept it locked. It is cool and dark and has a strange smell. As my eyes get used to the darkness, I make out the shape of tombs and crosses carved in stone. Father Abraham lights a candle and our shadows shiver on the walls. He leads me to a corner where there is a deep hole and a huge block of stone poking through the earth. If it was upright, it would be three times taller than me.

'This stele has lain here for two thousand years,' Father Abraham whispers. 'It is from the ancient Aksumite kingdom. We believe it is dedicated to the moon god.'

He holds the candle closer. Carved into the stone is a crescent moon and an inscription.

It looks like the writing on the golden disc.

'We have discovered other treasures from this great kingdom,' Father Abraham says. 'A perfume bottle, some pottery, a glass-beaded necklace and a bracelet of pink crystal. Many human skeletons have been found here, too – huge men with thick bones and great skulls. Some must have been giants, fierce warriors who died in battle. All of them have been taken to the museum in Addis Ababa so that everyone can share in their beauty and their mystery. We must marvel at these ancestors of ours. They are our history.'

'But where is the temple?' I say.

'Under our feet,' says Father Abraham.

'Do you think there may be other treasures there?' I ask.

Father Abraham smiles. 'Of that, I am certain.'

I feel a terrible guilt. What would Father Abraham think if he knew I had already taken one of those treasures?

I set off for the hill the next morning at least two hours before I am needed at the church. This time, I bring my bag and torch. I pass villagers along the road carrying great bundles on their backs. It is barely light. Trees are dark giants against the indigo sky.

Away from the houses, I start the steep climb. From down below comes the sound of a cockerel crowing. I can see it, perched on an iron roof. The village is waking.

I find my way easily, even in the half-light. The pile of branches is exactly where I left it. I get to work digging deeper and wider and faster. This time I am using a thicker, sharper stick which rips through the earth. When my arms grow tired I sit back and sift carefully through the heap of soil. Beetles scuttle over my fingers and flies buzz around my head. But all I find are stones and dust.

Deeper and deeper I go. Sweat is running down my cheeks and dripping on to the ground. I smile as

I imagine digging so much that I make a tunnel all the way to Father Abraham's temple.

The sun has risen now and the sounds of voices drift up from the village. There must be another pointer and another disc buried here somewhere, but after one more hour of digging, all I have found is a piece of charcoal and a clay bead. I sit down to rest and drink.

A goat is nibbling thorns from a bush nearby. I throw it a piece of bread and it trots towards me. Its ears flap as it chews. It sniffs the ground looking for more. I throw another piece which lands near its hoof and, as it is picking it up, there next to it is something small and black. I jump up and run towards it.

'Oh, little goat! Look what you have found!'

It is a black pointer, exactly like the first one, except it is longer. My heart is racing and I am fizzing inside. All I need now is to find the smaller disc.

The goat stands close, flicking its ears and tail, but as soon as I push the stick into the ground it bleats and trots away.

'Where are you going?' I say. 'Stay here. You bring me good luck.'

But the goat is not listening and I watch it disappear around the hill.

What if it is right? If I have not found anything here, perhaps I should try digging somewhere else.

I bundle up my belongings and find the goat round the other side, nodding its head as if it is expecting me.

From here, I can see the ladders still leaning against the church wall. I start to burrow into the hill. My heart is banging in my ears and my shoulders are shaking with effort. I am so glad that there is a cooler breeze on this side.

I stop to drink. The goat is still here, nudging me with its soft nose. I stroke its head.

'If I find treasure here,' I tell it, 'I promise I will give you a feast.'

It is exciting to be digging for treasure and it is even more exciting to find it as the sky is glowing like gold above the hills. I see the edge of something dark and solid. I break off clumps of soil and feel two curved edges. Two? Does this mean there are three golden discs? I am breathing fast now and trembling all over. I tunnel further in, heaving out great stones and handfuls of soil. Finally, I am able to reach into the space and ease out two discs and a long, twisted black pointer. I lay them out, side by side, and stare.

The largest disc is attached to a sort of base so I can stand it upright on the ground and there is a bolt at the centre and tiny pictures etched around it. One is shaped like a sword. Another looks like a pile of coins, there is a dark sun hiding behind a bright moon, then some wheat and a strange, curved boat with a mast. Further around, I see a skull. As I lift the disc and tilt it, I notice some tiny cogs through a small hole in the back. Maybe the cogs are there to move the pointers. The other disc is the smallest of the three with more of the strange script around the edge.

'Oh, little goat,' I say, 'I am going to give you the best green beans and freshest banana leaves you have ever tasted!'

3

Halo

I wake up after midday again. That's what it's like in the holidays. You stay up later and later and never see the mornings until you go back to school. Gran's in her wheelchair in the back garden.

'Morning, Gran,' I say.

I take my muesli into the sunshine. Gran dozes. I see the crimson bruises on her hands. The blue veins criss-crossing under her paper-thin skin. I think of heaven and wonder where it is.

Love you, Gran, I say in my head.

My phone's ringing. Mum waves it by the back door.

Jade, she mouths.

'You can say it out loud, Mum – she can't hear you.'

Jade's just back from a holiday in Italy and asks if she can come over.

* * *

We go up to my room. Her skin's the colour of toffee and her hair's tinged with highlights. We stand on the bed and look out of the window.

'Who's the new lad?' she says.

'You've seen him?'

'I waved. He was at the window.'

'He's called Pedro.'

'Ooo, exotic. Where's he from?'

'All over.'

'What d'you mean?'

'He's lived in different places.'

'International. I like that. Let's go and see him.'

She asks to use the toilet and comes out wearing eyeliner. I've never seen her in make-up before. She looks so grown up.

'Like it?' she says. 'Bought it on holiday.' She hooks her arm in mine. 'Come on, you,' she says.

We ring the bell and Pedro's sister comes to the door. She stares at us for ages with brown eyes full of sadness.

'Is Pedro in?' says Jade, like she's known him her whole life.

Pedro's sister calls up to him in another

language. He flops down the stairs. He looks surprised to see us.

Jade puts her hands on her hips. 'I'm Jade,' she says. 'Want to come out for a bit?'

Pedro smiles.

'I'll show you the village,' she says.

'OK.'

'Get your shoes on then,' says Jade.

We trek up the hill to the parish church. Pedro shoves his hands in his pockets and takes long strides.

'What were you speaking?' Jade asks.

'Spanish,' he says.

'Do you like my tan?'

Pedro shrugs. 'Guess so,' he says.

We head towards the newsagents and turn right. Jade leads the way.

'Let's start at one end and walk to the other,' she says.

We follow like a couple of silly ducklings. We pass the White Lion pub and the bakery, then Goosecroft Lane and Hill House Edge.

'This is where the village starts,' says Jade. She's standing by the sign.

Pedro's gazing in the other direction.

'What's up there?' he says.

'Pockley Moor,' I say.

'Is it far?'

'A mile or so.'

'What's that in kilometres?'

I think hard. 'About one point six?'

'What's the view like?'

'Best I've ever seen.'

'I want to see Pockley Moor,' says Pedro.

'Hold on, who's doing this tour?' says Jade. She's got her hands on her hips now and she's frowning. 'Come on, you lot. Follow me.'

She leads us back through the village and points out the Craven Arms hotel, the Hotchpotch shop, the primary school. We wave to Irene Siddle in the chippie and grumpy Donald Spud in the Spar. The sun's burning our shoulders so we stop at Mrs Clegg's to buy cold drinks.

'This the new lad then?' she says. She folds her arms across her gigantic bosom.

'Pedro Ortega,' he says. 'Pleased to meet you.'

He stretches to shake hands and Mrs Clegg blushes and grins.

'Well, aren't we polite?' she says. 'Wish everyone was as polite as you. Here – have a toffee twist.'

Pedro grins and pockets the sweet, then takes three cokes from the fridge and drops some coins into Mrs Clegg's hand. We head out into the dazzling summer day again.

There's a bunch of kids on Facebook Bench doing the usual stuff – scrolling, Instagramming, tossing back their heads and howling with laughter. We sit for a while and guzzle down our drinks.

'So that was Main Street,' says Jade. 'I'll show you my house next. We're at the . . . what you might call . . . *nicer* end of the village.'

Jade's dad bought a whole field for a million. Their house is easily the biggest in Thribbleston and quite possibly the whole of West Yorkshire. She takes us through the massive front door, side-glancing Pedro to check his reaction.

'What d'you think of the views?' she says.

Pedro gazes into the distance. 'They're a long way away,' he says.

I have to bite my lip to stop myself from grinning.

'Come on, I'll show you the garden,' she says. 'We're having a pool next summer.'

Jade's mum and dad are in the conservatory arguing about something. Her mum's face is bright pink and her dad's wagging a finger. He jabs her shoulder and she throws her hands in the air.

'Take no notice. They're always like that,' says Jade. She pushes us outside and we lounge on the deck chairs. 'So, come on, mystery man, what's your story? What brought you to the middle of nowhere?'

Pedro looks uneasy. He jumps up. He glances over at me.

'Anything else to see in the village?' he says.

'The library,' I say.

Jade sighs. 'Do we have to?'

'Do you want to, Pedro?'

'Sure,' he says.

Jade sniffs. 'Full of crappy books and a bunch of old fogies.'

She expects us to laugh but we don't, so we head out again, Jade leading us towards the play park.

'This has to be the most boring village in the entire country,' she says.

We stare at the rusty swings and the ancient

roundabout and the climbing frame.

'Look at it! This is all we've got for entertainment.'

We jump on the roundabout. We get it spinning so fast we can barely hold on.

'Let's do something mad,' Jade screams. 'Let's walk into the Craven Arms and order champagne.'

'We're not old enough for champagne,' I shout back.

'*Not old enough.*' She imitates me in a whining voice. 'Holy moly! There's got to be something more exciting than this.'

'Swings!' I shout, and we scramble across the grass. We stand on them, lean back, work them hard until we're horizontal.

'Where did you live before here?' Jade yells to Pedro.

'Switzerland,' he says.

'Can you ski?'

'Yeah. Love skiing.'

'Me, too. You ever been, Halo?'

She knows I haven't. She's just saying it to show me up.

The swings slow and we jump off. Jade makes a sudden move towards Pedro. She cups a hand around his ear and whispers something. He scowls and shakes his head. I have a horrible feeling it's something about me. Pedro's hands are back in his pockets now. He's shrugging and kicking the ground. Then he turns suddenly.

'Got to go! See you later!' he shouts.

He half waves then crosses the grass and hops over a wall. He's heading for Main Street.

'Why are you going?' I shout, but he pretends not to hear. I turn to Jade. 'What did you say to him?'

'Nothing you need know about. Anyway, I'm getting my hair done on Saturday, want to come?'

I imagine her in a swivel chair being fussed over and me having to sit there watching.

Jade whines. 'Ah, come on, don't be so boring.'

I only have seconds to answer. Any longer and she'll know I don't want to.

'I have to ask Mum,' I say. 'Anyway, we're probably going for a walk on the moors.'

'Who's we?'

'Mum and Dad.' I'm going to ask Pedro – but I won't tell Jade that. In any case, she doesn't even like the moors.

'You're walking with *parents*?' She's folding her arms now. 'Come on, you'll have far more fun with me.'

There's something in her eyes, as if she's pleading with me.

'Right,' I say. 'What time's your appointment?'

'Twelve,' she says.

'I'll come for half an hour. Then I'll have to go.'

'Half an hour? Don't bother, then. *Honestly*, Halo, I don't know what's got into you. It's like you don't care any more.' And she turns and sets off towards home.

I walk back down Kirkby Road. I see Pedro in the distance, his long legs, the swing of his arms. My eyes are watering and I don't want him to see me like this, so I slow down and watch him disappear into his house.

Back home, I clean up my face but Gran knows there's something wrong. She wheels her chair next to me.

'The world is full of trouble,' she says.

'The world was fine before people arrived. It's *people* who're trouble.'

Gran sighs. 'Bet I know who.'

I look at her. 'I don't want to talk about it.' I feel bad, like I'm pushing Gran away, so I get up and kiss her on her cheek. 'I'm going to the library,' I say. 'Please tell Mum.'

4

Ageze

It is hard to explain what it looks like. You have to see it for yourself. How can I describe it?

Magnificent?

Magical?

Yes, I am sure there is magic in it somewhere.

I am back home in Addis Ababa. Ma is cooking. My sisters are playing with dolls and prams outside and here I am in my room with the blinds pulled down, a chair against the door and three discs and three pointers spread out over my desk.

My hands are trembling. I can barely believe they are here in front of me.

I have cleaned the soil from each piece with water and soft cloths, pulling out bits of leaves and dead insects from the cogs. The discs are gleaming now and the symbols and writing are clear and bright. Slowly and with great care, I slide each disc and its pointer on to the bolt attached to the largest disc. They slot together perfectly with the pointers moving smoothly in between. As the discs are different sizes, the symbols can be seen around the edge of each one.

Now I must find a way to make it work. There is a small hole in the back, shaped like a triangle. If I could make a handle or a key, perhaps I could wind it up?

I try gluing match sticks together but it is hard to cut them into the right shape to fit the hole. Either they are not long enough or they snap. I must find something stronger.

I remember watching Da's friend, Abdi, at the printing works, oiling the machines and fixing them when they broke down. Abdi can make just about anything. Maybe he could make me a key?

I measure the depth of the hole with a piece of straight wire and a ruler, then trace its shape and mark the measurements on a piece of paper. I am hoping that the printing works is still open.

I lift the Device into my cupboard and pile T-shirts over it.

I call to Ma. 'I am going out!'

'Where are you going?'

'To see Abdi.'

'Why have you suddenly thought of Abdi? You have not been there in months.'

'I would just like to see him.' I am sure that did not sound convincing.

Ma peeps round the door.

'Do not bother Abdi too much while he is working,' she says. 'But say hello from me.'

I race to the front door.

'And be back in one hour. No more,' she shouts.

'Yes, Ma!' I say.

I love the noises when you walk into the building. The printing press sounds like a wheezy old man, gasping and sighing as the papers are pressed on to inky letters and fall into neat piles.

Abdi has worked here for years and years. He oils the cogs and replaces the rollers and washers when they wear out. I put my head around the door and see him in his blue overalls, turning handles and pressing levers. I stand and watch for a while. Everyone is concentrating and I do not want to interrupt them.

I edge closer and Abdi turns around. He smiles

when he sees me and his eyes twinkle inside a mound of little creases. He holds up a hand.

'Wait a minute.' He waves for another worker to come and look after his printing press, then he comes over.

'How are you, young man? What brings you here today?'

'I wanted to ask for your help,' I say. 'I need to make a special key.' I show him my drawing.

'This is an unusual shape,' he says. 'What is the key for?'

I pause. 'I do not know yet, but it is something very important.'

'Important enough for you to come to see your old friend?' He studies the triangle shape, and the numbers. 'Are these the exact measurements?'

'I measured it very carefully,' I say.

'It must be exact for a key to fit properly. Leave it with me and I will see what I can do.'

'Thank you so much!'

I watch the printed sheets gliding off the press. On a table are piles of little books, small and thick with red and green covers. Abdi tells me they are Bibles. He picks one up and opens it.

The writing looks like the letters on the Device.

'These are our best sellers,' he says. 'As soon as we print them, they are sold out.'

'What language is this?' I say.

'It is the ancient language of Ge'ez. It is more than two thousand years old.'

'I have heard of Ge'ez at school. Can you read it?'

'I read it from my Bible,' say Abdi, 'and I know that I am talking to God, but I do not understand exactly what each word is saying.'

'If I show you some letters, would you be able to tell me if they are Ge'ez and what they mean?'

Abdi shakes his head. 'I am sorry. It is an old, old language once spoken and understood by everyone in this country. Now it is only spoken in worship and prayer.' He holds up a finger. 'But there is someone who may able to help you.'

'Who?' I say.

'A monk, a scribe – a *meri gheta*. He works in the Patriarchate Museum. You should go there and ask for his help.'

'Thank you. I will. When should I come back for the key?'

'In three days, my friend. It will be ready then.'

I am smiling my widest smile and we shake hands like proper business men.

'Give my regards to your ma and da.'

'Thank you, Abdi! I will!'

Three days later, I pick up the key. It is perfect.

I hug Abdi then race back home, fly through the front door and kick off my shoes.

'My goodness! What is all the rush?' cries Ma.

'Sorry,' I say. I stroll through the kitchen and into my bedroom. I have to look casual or Ma will be even more suspicious. She seems to have special radar powers when anything secret is happening.

I put my chair against the door.

Here is the brass key on the palm of my hand. It is two centimetres long with three equal, straight sides – like an elongated triangle. Abdi has made it well. It feels strong between my fingers.

I am sitting on my bedroom floor looking at the Device. I turn it so I can see the slot at the back.

'Oh, noble and magnificent machine,' I whisper. 'I will now bring you to life and reveal your story.'

In my heart, I am hoping it will show me something amazing. Treasure, maybe? Or a mystery to solve?

But I must not expect too much. After all, it has been buried in the earth for thousands of years and has been put back together by a twelve-year-old boy who knows nothing about ancient devices.

I slide the triangular key into the slot and twist. It is stiff. I turn harder. Still it does not move. I push the key in further, turn it with more force. Something must be blocking it. I pull it out again.

Perhaps the shape is wrong.

Maybe the sides are not equal in length.

I turn the key once to the right and slot it in place. Still it refuses to move. Did I give Abdi the wrong measurements? Or did he make a mistake? Should I go back and ask him to make another key?

I turn the triangle once more to the right. This is the last position it can be in, the last chance to make it work. I push it back into the slot and this time it seems to connect and moves further inside. I take a deep breath and twist.

Yes! It is turning!

Gently and slowly, I wind clockwise, listening to clicks and whirrs from deep inside. I wind and wind until the key will not turn any more, then sit back and watch.

The pointers on each of the discs twitch suddenly and I jump and gasp. They start to swing this way and that, as if they are enjoying moving again. My eyes are wide and my heart is thudding. I move closer and listen to the sound it is making – *puff, puff, puff*, in and out, in and out – as if it is breathing.

I am trembling now. It feels like I am waking an ancient being. My shoulders are clenched around my ears. I watch and wait, staying perfectly still as if moving, even one finger, might distract it.

But nothing happens.

I pick it up and look at it. I am sure that it is wound up now, so what else does it need?

I turn it around, examining every curve and pointer, each disc and symbol. What have I missed? I look at the base on which the Device is sitting. There are four grooves on either side, all mottled and worn. Eight little furrows. Are they for decoration, or are they spaces for something?

Fingers, maybe?

I place my hands over the slots and immediately the pointer on the smallest disc twitches.

I jump as if I have been given an electric shock.

'Sorry, sorry,' I whisper. I breathe deeply.

'I was not expecting you to move. I am . . . going to try again.'

I know it is strange that I am talking to a piece of metal but I am starting to believe that, somehow, it can sense that I am here.

With my fingers resting in the grooves again, I force myself to stay calm. The pointer on the smallest disc shivers. *Click, click*, it begins to glide, once around the disc, twice, then it stops on a symbol.

What is it waiting for?

I listen to the cogs ticking. It reminds me of my teacher, Mrs Bezu, tapping her fingernails on the desk when she is waiting for something. Maybe the Device is waiting for me to write down the symbol? I pick up a pen and copy it down.

As soon my fingers are back on the grooves, the black arrow twitches, pauses, then goes again, slipping forwards and backwards, then forwards again.

Each time it pauses, I write down the symbol.

𝝽𝝽 𝝽 𝝽𝝽𝝽𝝽

𝝽𝝽 𝝽𝝽

The Device stops.

And sighs.

Carefully, I slide my fingers from the grooves and heave in a deep breath.

My head is spinning with questions now. I get up and pace around the room, trying to feel calmer.

What sort of device knows that I am touching it?

What if I have dug up a kind of ancient magic?

Maybe it was buried in the ground for a good reason . . . because it is dangerous.

In all the stories I have read, stealing treasure has never turned out well. Perhaps I should return it to Father Abraham's church.

Or maybe, if it can do good things, I could help people.

I sit down at the table again. The moment I place my fingers on the grooves, the pointer on the middle disc springs into life. It moves quickly, pausing for me to scribble down each symbol, before it spins and pauses again.

ፗ፟ፘ

ፙ ፚ ፛

፜ ፝ ፞

But I have no idea what they mean.

What about the largest disc? There are tiny engravings all around the edge. Some of them are easy to recognise: a sword, three suns, an eclipse, and something that could be a volcano. My fingers are still resting on the grooves as the pointer nudges around the big disc, forwards, then back, then forwards again, feeling its way. Now it is ticking along stealthily, searching for something, as if it has eyes and is scanning the engravings. The pointer shivers over a symbol deciding whether it is the right one, flicks from side to side like it is shaking its head, then clicks once again, and stops.

All is still.

I slip my fingers from the grooves.

It is pointing to a symbol with three wavy lines.

I decide to treat this as an experiment. I find a notebook, write down today's date and draw all the symbols that the Device has shown me. I will wind it up and look for patterns. Cause and effect. That is what a proper scientist would do. But to truly understand what the symbols mean, I must go to the Patriarchate Museum and find the *meri gheta*.

NINE...

5

Halo

The library is my sanctuary. I choose a book and sit at my usual table in the front left corner. If someone's there I stand near them until they leave.

But today, there is no one.

My two favourite things are reading and thinking.

Reading is a kind of magic because books make worlds in your head. I'm totally convinced that I actually teleport inside each story and even when I've finished, I can close my eyes and go back to that world as if it's a living, breathing place.

When I'm thinking, I sit with a finger on the corner of my mouth and stare out of the window. Whatever's in front of me disappears for a while as I imagine galaxies or the International Space Station whirling around the Earth at five miles per second. In fact, that's what I'm doing right now except I keep thinking of questions like, *why am I still friends with Jade?*

The sun shines through the window and warms my face. Mrs Moira Hattersley is gliding around in her flowery dress. She's the librarian and tells you off if you don't say her name properly. I think it's because she has to have everything exact, so if you just say 'Moira' or 'Mrs Hattersley' she thinks it could mean someone else.

Mrs Moira Hattersley gives me a wave. I'm in here so often I should have a frequent visitor's card. She has a little room at the back where she disappears every now and then. When I was younger, I thought she lived there. She knows every single book on the shelves like she's a living, breathing catalogue system, and she's tremendously thoughtful because she puts the books for young and noisy children in a bright, cheerful but *separate* room, with a door. If I had to choose a second mum, it would be Mrs Moira Hattersley.

I raise my hand as if she's a teacher and she comes over.

'What can I help you with, my dear?'

'Is there a computer available, Mrs Moira

Hattersley?'

She smiles because I said her name correctly. 'Abso-blooming-lutely,' she says.

I follow her into the little room at the back.

'Help yourself,' she says.

The room's completely empty.

I've been wanting to google him for ages but it seemed sneaky doing it at home, especially as I can actually see him across the road in his bedroom. Using the library computer makes it more like research, rather than stalking.

In any case, it turns out there are about a billion Pedro Ortegas on the planet, most of them living in South America, Spain or the United States. If I want to know more about Pedro, I'll have to ask him myself.

He's up in his room when I get home, sitting at his computer. He sees me and swings open the window.

'Want to go to Pockley Moor tomorrow?' I yell.

His eyes widen. ''Course,' he says.

'Afternoon?'

'Perfect.'

'Bring a picnic.'

'OK.'

'And some comfy shoes.'

I hesitate. I want to ask him what Jade was whispering in the park but I decide I don't care any more.

'See you then,' I say.

And Pedro waves and pulls the window closed again.

6

Ageze

An old man is sitting in a darkened room. He wears a cloth around his head and glasses on the tip of his nose. All I can hear is his pen scratching on paper. I hardly dare to breathe.

A click in the corridor. Footsteps, then whispers. It must be the security men looking for me. I am not supposed to be in this part of the museum. I step further inside the room and press myself against a bookcase. It stretches as high as the ceiling and along every wall.

'If you come over here, they will not find you.' His voice is soft as if it has not been used for centuries. 'Quickly, young man, or you will be in trouble.'

I slip past the books and the glass display cases to where the old man is crouched over a desk.

'Did you arrive here by accident or with intention?' he breathes.

'I paid one *birr* to enter the Patriarchate Museum but I may have lost my way.'

The old man waits as if he knows this is not the whole truth.

'I was looking for something.'

'What were you looking for?' This time he glances up and I see the deep wrinkles on his face and the milky blueness of his eyes.

I pull out a piece of paper from my pocket and unfold it.

'I am looking for someone who can tell me what these mean.'

He grips the paper and studies it. His hands tremble.

'This script is two thousand years old.' His finger trails over the beautiful shapes. He hums and nods. 'This language was once the spoken tongue of our ancient land.'

We hear whispering again, footsteps outside. The old man's watery eyes fix on mine. 'Step behind here,' he says, 'and keep very still.'

He waves to the curtains that hang from ceiling to floor. Behind them are manuscripts and scrolls and ancient books. I tuck in my feet and hold my breath.

'We are sorry to disturb you, *Meri Gheta*. We saw a boy come this way. He should not have left the main part of the museum. Have you seen him?'

'Do not worry. If I find a boy who is lost I will show him the way back. Make sure that the door to the corridor is locked. It is important that I remain undisturbed.'

'Of course, *Meri Gheta*.'

The men leave and all is quiet again. I step out into the darkened room.

'Come and sit with me,' he says.

On his desk is a pot of ink, a bamboo pen and pages of black silky writing.

'I will tell you the meaning of the script, if you will help me to arrange these books and manuscripts on the shelves,' he says.

He points to a dark corner where there are jumbled piles spread across the floor.

'I agree,' I say. 'May I tidy them now?'

The old man smiles.

'Arranging them correctly will take time, and it must be done with great patience and care. You must first ask your mother and your father if you can come here. If they are in agreement, you may enter by the side door tomorrow at thirty minutes past four o'clock.'

'Thank you, *Meri Gheta*. This is very kind of you.' I pause. I do not want to leave without knowing what the Device was showing me. 'Do you think you could tell me what some of the symbols mean? Today?'

I glance at my piece of paper and he narrows his eyes as he studies it. I listen to the soft wheezing in his chest. He leans forward, takes his pen and begins to write.

'These,' he says, drawing his finger across my notes, 'are letters.' He writes down N and E. 'And this is the number fifteen.'

'But what do they mean?' I say. 'Fifteen what?'

'I am sorry, young man, but I cannot help you with that.'

I wonder if I will to be able to work it out myself. If I cannot, I will never know what the Device is telling me.

'And these?' I point to the symbols shown on the middle disc. 'If it is not too much to ask,' I add.

The *meri gheta* scans the paper. 'These are all numbers,' he says. He scratches them on to the paper.

2 8 0 6 2 0 1 8

13 17

I stare at them for a while.

'Do they mean anything to you?' asks the *meri gheta*.

'I am not sure. I think it could be a date. And, perhaps, a time. And if that is right, it is tomorrow.'

The *meri gheta* looks again. 'This is possible,' he says.

So what is the Device doing? Is it warning me of something?

'*Meri Gheta*, if you do not mind, there is one more symbol that I would like to show you.' I point to the three wavy lines. 'Could you tell me what you think this means?'

His brow tightens into furrows and his eyes dart from side to side as if he has been suddenly disturbed by something. He takes a breath and tries to smile.

'This is neither a letter nor a number in Ge'ez,' he says. 'Have you thought that it may represent a river or the sea?'

'Yes,' I say. 'That is exactly what I thought. I think it could mean water.'

He suddenly gets to his feet. 'You will excuse me now, young man. I must resume my work.' He shuffles towards the door. 'I will show you where you may enter next time.'

'Thank you,' I say.

We follow a corridor that leads to the back of the museum. He shields his eyes as he opens the door into the bright sunshine.

'Do not forget to ask permission from your mother and your father,' he says. 'I will be here at this door at thirty minutes past four o'clock tomorrow. Do not be late.'

I race through the museum gardens back to the main entrance and into the busy street, trying to work out what N and E and 15 could mean, and what they have to do with water.

Whatever it is, will happen tomorrow.

The twenty-eighth of June, two thousand and eighteen.

I think the Device is predicting something.

I am still awake at midnight. After Ma and Da have gone to sleep, I tiptoe out of the house and sit on the steps near the front gate. Under the starry sky, cars are buzzing along and dogs are barking. There is a *thump*, *thump*, *thump* of reggae music somewhere. My stomach is tight as I scan the darkness.

Doubts creep into my head. What if I am wrong? What if the numbers and letters mean something else? The *meri gheta* seemed sure that the wavy lines mean water but I am a long way from the Akaki River and miles away from the sea. And there has not been rain here for months.

I think about the Device again. If the symbols on the big disc show 'what' is going to happen, and the small disc with numbers shows 'when', could the middle disc be showing 'where'? Are N and E directions? And, if that is correct, how far is '15'? Metres? Kilometres?

I go inside for my compass and walk fifteen metres in a north-east direction from my bedroom, where the Device was when it made the prediction. It takes me across the road to the skatepark where I play with Yared, Addisu and Natty. We are here almost every day after school and sometimes all day during the holidays. Maybe somewhere around here the 'something to do with water' is going to happen.

It is hard to keep my eyes open. I go back inside and flop on to my bed.

The next thing I know I am being woken by Ma's voice.

'Time you were awake, Ageze.'

I jump up. 'Has anything happened yet?'

'What are you expecting?' Her hands are on her hips, which is never a good sign. 'It is ten o'clock already. I think you must be growing again. You always sleep too much when you are growing. Breakfast?'

'Yes, Ma. I think I will eat outside.' I know there are three hours to go but I feel like I need to keep watch.

While Ma is cooking, I scan the news to see if anyone is predicting a monsoon or a flood or a tsunami. And I take a peek out of the front door at the skatepark.

Just in case.

7

Halo

The sun's beating down the next morning. The weather lady says it's going to be a scorcher. The ice cream van is playing 'Teddy Bear's Picnic' and the song brings Norman out.

'Summa's 'ere! Summa's 'ere! Summa's 'ere!' shouts Norman.

When I was little I used to call him 'the shouting boy' because that's what he did. But I don't call him that now. He was in a terrible car accident when he was six and has something called an 'acquired brain injury', which means he yells sometimes and gets muddled and needs a bit of help. I let him go in front of me because he's not good at queuing.

'Ninety-nine! Ninety-nine! Ninety-nine!' he shouts.

The ice cream man passes him a cone dripping with red goo. Norman forgets to pay.

'You need to give him your money, Norman,' I say.

He brings coins from his pocket and I help him count them out. He licks the ice cream.

'Summa's 'ere! Summa's 'ere! Summa's 'ere!' he shouts and we do a high five before he heads back to his mum, Jean Fitchett, waiting by the door.

I've been sent to get three Mister Softees so we can sit in the back garden and pretend we're at the seaside. Gran's idea. She can tell something's bothering me and I think she's trying to cheer me up. Mum's getting her a bowl of warm water for her feet (pretend sea) and a tartan rug (pretend sand).

'Just the job,' says Gran. 'Just as good as Scarborough.'

We sit back in the stripy deck chairs. The sun's scorching and the ice creams are starting to drip.

'*Summer is the time to take charge*,' says Mum. She's reading her horoscope. '*You feel unusually energised. Pisces and Aquarius are in alignment, indicating a windfall.*' Mum jiggles her eyebrows and mouths, 'EuroMillions,' like it's bad luck to say it out loud. '*Beware the fiery nature of the cosmos when a momentous event will befall you.'*

'What's going to fall on you?' says Gran.

'Let's wait and see,' says Mum.

'Jade's mum and dad were having a row,' I say. It's not related to anything we've been talking about and I'm quite surprised I just blurted it out like that.

'Crumbs,' says Mum. 'When?'

'Yesterday.'

'Is Jade all right?' she asks. 'Maybe you should ask her to come and stay?'

'Maybe,' I say.

'Her mum and dad probably need a bit of time on their own, that's all.'

I sit a while, wondering why my mum and dad don't argue. I've never seen them even close to a row. Sometimes Mum'll say, 'Come on, Tony, pick up those socks,' when Dad uses his right big toe to peel off his left sock and his left big toe to peel off his right sock and leaves them under the table. And sometimes Dad tuts when Mum's taking ages with her mascara. But he's never cross about Gran living with us, even when she's done one of her five-day poos and stunk the house out and we're dashing around madly to open all the windows.

Maybe they just argue in private.

'There's no space anyway,' I say. 'What with Gran in the spare room and the little room packed with junk.'

But Mum's drying Gran's feet and isn't listening.

There's a breeze now, all cool and fresh. A plane rumbles overhead.

'That's enough of Scarborough for this morning.' Mum pushes Gran's wheelchair up the slope and into the conservatory. 'Halo, I'm keeping an eye on Norman this afternoon while his mum gets her hair done. Can you help out?'

'I wish I could but I'm going on the expedition,' I say.

'Of course,' says Mum. 'I forgot. Did you invite Jade?'

'No,' I say. 'It's just Pedro and me.'

It's boiling in the afternoon. Mum's lathering me in sunscreen.

'Hat, sunglasses, water,' she says. 'Got your phone?'

'Yep.'

'Fully charged?'

'Yep. I also have a first-aid kit, an emergency beacon and my zombie apocalypse survival kit.'

'Don't be cheeky,' says Mum.

She crams a sandwich box, two bananas and a bag of dried apricots into my backpack. I hold my breath in case she notices the torches I've already put in there.

'Call me at three,' she says.

'Wilco.'

'And if you reach Leeds you've gone too far.'

'You're joking.'

''Course I am,' she says. 'Any funny business and you come straight back home.'

'Define "funny business".'

Mum rolls her eyes and points me to the door.

'And keep to the paths,' she shouts after me. 'No wading through heather. There's hidden boulders. And adders. And keep your socks pulled up – you don't want to get bitten by ticks and get that what-d'you-call-it?'

'Lyme disease,' I shout back.

Pedro's on the front lawn in shorts and trainers.

Not a sign of sunscreen or a hat.

Mum waves.

'Look after each other,' she says.

We head up the hill to the church. It's the first time I've been up here without Mum and Dad. It feels like I'm stepping off the edge of the world. I race along the road waving my arms and kicking my legs. I look back at Pedro and see the dimples in his cheeks as he smiles.

We follow dry-stone walls, see them arching and slumping over the fields. Clouds huddle behind the great stretch of moorland.

'What's it like in winter?' says Pedro.

'Freezing,' I say. 'And beautiful. One January when the roads were closed, Dad brought me all the way up here and we carved a huge toboggan run that ended up by the White Hart. It was magic. All the kids in the village had a go and when it was getting dark we put torches and candles to light the way.'

'We've got to do that again,' says Pedro. 'Promise?'

'Cross my heart,' I say.

The moor is a hotchpotch of purple heather, rusty bracken and pale yellow grass. The wind is wild and the sun burns down on us. This is a place that invites you to run, so that's what we do. We sprint down grassy pathways, hurdle clumps of heather and strange carved rocks. Race so hard that we're sure if we spread our arms we'd take off and fly.

I grab his hand and we tear along like champion fell runners until we're up on Grubbit's Scar looking down at the sparkling, winding river and the little town of Skeldale below.

'There's something I want to show you,' I say.

'What is it?' says Pedro.

'It's an absolute secret. Promise you'll tell no one.'

'Cross my heart,' he says.

There's a steep climb up on to High Crag, over boulders and moss and thick stubbly grass. Sheep scatter out of our way. Skylarks warble high above. We collapse at the top and wait to get our breath back. It's only when we're on our feet again and over the hill that we can hear it.

Pedro turns and looks at me. 'Awesome,' he says.

He hasn't even seen it yet.

It's hard to scramble down the path, dangerous almost. We're grabbing tussocks of grass to steady ourselves. Pedro poses by an ancient tree so twisted and gnarled it looks like someone put a spell on it. He bends himself into some sort of weird shape and I snap him on my phone.

There's a warning notice: 'DANGER. Slippery slope. Do not enter the water at any time.' Mum would have a fit if she knew we were here. We follow a thin path along the brown, churning river. The water is full of froth and spray is falling in tiny droplets on our arms and faces. Then there it is, towering in front of us. We have to shout over the roar.

'Ingilby Foss!'

'It's amazing!'

'Knew you'd like it!'

Rusty brown water thunders over Whin Sill and falls as a white bubbling mass into the deep pool below. It has us transfixed like we're under its spell.

I move closer so Pedro can hear.

'Don't be thinking of going in there. Three lads drowned not long ago. They were all good swimmers but it was the cold that got them. So never be tempted, OK?' I glare at him and he nods and smiles. 'Actually, this isn't the secret.'

'There's something else?'

'Everyone knows about the waterfall. I'm taking you somewhere that no one knows about.'

We make our way under the trees to where the water is calmer and rocks lie higgledy-piggledy and where we can hear each other again.

'We'll have to leave our backpacks. How are you with small spaces?'

Pedro shrugs. 'Let's find out.'

The boulders are green and slippery. I show him where to put his feet and which branches to hold on to. We're heading up the side of the waterfall where you have to squeeze between tree trunks and boulders, where only the most determined and brave ever venture. I'm telling myself all this as we climb because I'm petrified one of us might fall.

'This rock's nearly three hundred million years old,' I say. 'It's really hard but underneath there's limestone. And where there's limestone, there are caves.'

Pedro helps me pull away the branches that

cover the entrance. He hasn't said anything yet and I'm wondering if scrambling up perilous rock faces and squeezing into hidden caves are the sort of everyday things you do when you're at boarding school in the Swiss Alps. Then I see his blue and brown eyes twinkle and his smile all wide and lovely.

'How did you find it?' he asks.

'By chance.'

We're shining our torches now as we squeeze through the gap and drop on to the cave floor. The walls glisten and pale stunted fingers hang, mini stalactites dripping from the roof.

'Whoa, Halo Moon! You are full of surprises.'

He's touching the walls and the floor. He's gazing everywhere, into each corner and each crevice. For a while we just sit, listening to the rumble of the waterfall.

We go back a way I've never been before. We've completely forgotten about lunch so we find a spot looking over Grimbalds reservoir and the hills where Yorkshire cyclists Billy Howarth and Tom Billingsly slog up and down. We sink into the soft grass and ferns.

Pedro takes out a pork pie and half a tub of hummus and a bag of crisps – like that was all they had in the fridge and no one had been shopping. I give him one of my sandwiches and a banana.

'What does your sister do?' I say.

'She's called Carmela. She wants to be a doctor.'

'Must be clever then.'

He nods. 'Pretty smart.'

My phone alarm goes off. It's 2:59.

'Time to connect to the mother ship,' I say. 'I'll tell her I've broken my leg and you've got sunstroke and we're totally lost.'

Pedro grins and shakes his head. 'You're crazy.'

'Good crazy?'

He nods. 'Very good crazy.'

I'm trying not to smile but there's a buzz in my stomach and my heart's beating wildly.

'Hello, Mum. Yes, everything's fine. Yes, we have eaten and we're going to walk back now. No zombies and no adders. Yes, Mum. Over and out.'

We head back towards Moor Road where we walked three hours ago – a whole three hours that I've spent with Pedro Ortega, just me and him, the mysterious new boy whose bedroom is diagonally opposite mine, who's lived everywhere and done everything, who lay down beside me to watch the stars and the meteors a million miles away.

EIGHT . . .

8

Ageze

I am sitting on the steps near the front gate. There are many people walking to and from the market. Many cars rushing along the street.

I am waiting for the 'something' to happen. If I have understood the Device, whatever the 'something' is will take place in the skatepark.

Every shout or beep of a horn makes me leap up and race to the gate.

It is ten past one. Yared is there in the distance with his skateboard under his arm.

'Yared!' I jump down the steps, sprint through the gate and over the road.

He is already on his board shooting over ramps. He brakes and we high five.

'What's up?' he says.

'Something bad is going to happen. Here. In exactly six minutes.'

Yared is smiling. 'What are you talking about?'

'Do you trust me?'

''Course I do. What do you mean, something bad?'

'I do not know yet. Come over to my house. We will wait there.'

'Are you sure?'

'Yes, well, no. Maybe,' I say.

Yared laughs. 'I can wait six minutes for my best friend, but after that it is skateboard time!'

We are by the gate, watching. Yared is standing on his board.

'It must be six minutes now,' he says.

'Wait,' I say. I glance at my phone. 'Just a little longer.'

At exactly seventeen minutes past one, there is a rumbling sound. We feel it through our feet. We wait, standing perfectly still. There are no more rumbles for at least another minute. What is happening? My whole body is on red alert, heart beating fast, eyes scanning up and down, legs ready to charge.

We see two boys in the far corner on the other side of the road. It is Addisu and Natty, Yared's little brothers.

'Stop!' I yell. We wave to them. We race to the

roadside. A truck goes by, then a taxi. 'Come on! Come on!'

When it is clear we streak across. At that moment, the rumbling starts again, stronger and louder.

'Go back!' we yell to the boys. 'It is not safe here.'

They grin and wave. They cannot hear us. They are in the middle of the skatepark now, coming closer.

There is a sudden roar as something explodes.

Out of the rectangle of dusty, sun-baked earth comes a gigantic tower, a jet of water spurting metres into the air. Bits of stone and earth fall around us. Dogs are going crazy, drivers are tumbling out of their cars to see what is happening. Passers-by start to run, splashing through the water that is starting to pour down the road. As I run I see the spout growing higher and higher and the spray gushing wider, while underneath, the earth bulges and splits, and great cracks start to spread.

Addisu and Natty are right underneath it. They are on the ground, trapped by the force of the falling spray.

'Get them out!' I scream, and without hesitation we race into the bubbling torrent.

The force of the water is battering us so hard we can barely stand. Under our feet, the ground is crumbling and dissolving as huge chunks are carried away. Gulping in a deep breath, I fight my way through the cascade towards Addisu, who is still pinned to the ground, almost invisible inside the mass of frothing water. I am close to him now but the force is pushing me back. I see Yared rolling over to Natty. It seems easier than standing up or crawling. I do the same, launching myself on the ground, turning over and over until I am touching Addisu. Sharp stones dig into my arms and back, I am up on my knees, heaving his limp body from the ground and hauling him over my shoulder. The water is pounding down, slapping my head and making it impossible to see. I need to breathe. I am dizzy. Desperate for air.

A few more steps, just a little further.

I feel someone pulling me. Someone is lifting Addisu and dragging me backwards. My eyes are tightly closed. I am able to take little breaths now. Out of the water, I lie on my back listening to sirens and shouts, and then Yared's voice.

'They are fine,' he says, close to my ear. 'They are OK.'

A police car arrives. Then another.

'Everyone, move away from the water! Move away!' shouts the policeman.

The little boys are sitting up now. Their eyes are wide, watching the huge fountain gushing from the earth.

'Thank goodness,' I say. 'Thanks be to God.'

It is only when we are back on the steps in front of my house, drying off in the sun, that I truly realise what this means.

It works! The Device actually works!

'How did you know that was going to happen?' whispers Yared. 'Is it magic? Witchcraft?'

'I . . . I cannot say, not yet.' I wish I could tell him about the Device, but it feels impossible right now. Something is telling me that I must keep it hidden, at least until I find out what power it really has.

Ma stands on the steps, her arms around Natty and Addisu, watching the men fixing the burst water pipe.

'What a blessing you were both there,' she says to us. 'You should have your photograph in the newspaper. Local heroes. You will have a fan club in no time.'

Fixing the burst pipe takes hours. Yared and his brothers head back home and only a few curious children stay to watch until the spout of water has disappeared and the men have packed up their tools and driven away.

Even with all the excitement, I have not forgotten my very important appointment at the Patriarchate Museum. First, I must explain to Ma where I am going.

'With who?' she says. Her eyes are scrunched up tight.

'He is a monk at the museum. I think that he preserves ancient manuscripts by writing them out by hand. I said I would help him organise his books on the shelves.'

'How did you meet this *meri gheta*?' she asks.

'I went the wrong way in the museum.'

Ma takes in a deep breath. She waits.

'I sneaked into the forbidden part because I wanted to see what it was like, and when the *meri gheta* saw me he said if I helped he would not report me to the guards.'

'This is not something you would usually do,' says Ma. 'Sometimes you are far too inquisitive.'

'Please let me go, Ma! He said he would teach me.'

'Well, it will be educational I am sure, so you may go. But take your phone and answer if I call.'

'Yes, Ma,' I say. 'And thank you.'

Before I leave, I go over what I need to know to be able to use the Device.

It can predict things, I am sure of that now. If I learn the Ge'ez numbers I will be able to work out dates and distances, but I must also learn the Ge'ez letters for the compass directions: ደ ኢ ዐ ጥ

The picture symbols on the big disc may be more difficult to understand, so I copy some of them down. I really hope the *meri gheta* will be able to help me. I think I must understand all of them if I am to use the Device properly.

At exactly half past four, I arrive at the back of the Patriarchate Museum. The *meri gheta* seems pleased that I am on time. He locks the door behind me and I follow him to his room. He takes his usual seat.

'You will remember,' he says, 'that you are here to help me place these books and manuscripts in their correct positions on the shelves.'

I glance at the corner. The pile seems to have grown since yesterday.

'Yes, *Meri Gheta*,' I say. 'How will I know where to put them?'

'On the spine of each book there are numbers in Ge'ez.' He passes me a piece of parchment on which numerals and Ge'ez numbers are written side by side. 'You are a clever boy. I am sure that you will learn these quickly.'

Somehow, the bookcase seems even bigger than I remember. Twelve wide shelves and a tall wooden ladder up to the ceiling.

'*Meri Gheta*, before I start, I have something that I would like to ask you.'

I take the paper from my pocket and unfold it. On it are all the symbols that I copied from the largest disc.

'Could you please tell me what these mean?'

The room is so quiet I can hear his thumb rubbing

the paper as he studies it. He looks at me over his glasses. 'Tell me,' he says, 'where did you find these?'

Something in his eyes makes me nervous.

'I . . .'

'Have you been travelling lately?'

I shiver even though my heart is thumping. 'I stayed with my grandma.'

'In the north?'

'Yes, in the north.'

'And this is where you saw these symbols?'

'Yes, *Meri Gheta*.'

'Where exactly did you see them?'

I do not know what to tell him. If I say that I found them on an ancient Device that I dug up from near a church, a Device that predicts things, I am sure that he would demand to see it and maybe take it away from me.

'On . . .' I breathe, 'I saw them on . . . obelisks. Father Abraham showed me the tombs and stelae. I saw the symbols there, carved into stone.'

The *meri gheta* stares. 'And you saw all of these symbols carved on gravestones?'

'Yes. There were many tombs and the stelae are very tall.'

Please forgive me, God. I am so sorry for all this lying.

The *meri gheta* glances again at my paper. 'These are ancient symbols from the Aksumite kingdom. Let us take the symbol for water, which you showed me before.' He points to it on my paper. 'This could mean any of the sources of water that we have on Earth – rain, streams, lakes, rivers, seas, water from taps and from wells. Although there are some symbols here that have only one meaning.'

'Which ones?' I say.

'This, for example.' He points to the ears of wheat.

'Food?' I say.

The *meri gheta*'s eyes twinkle.

'I would like to start putting away the books now,' I say. 'Maybe, for every ten books I place correctly on the shelves, you could tell me what one symbol means?'

The *meri gheta*'s lips stretch into the smallest of smiles as he picks up his pen.

'Let us start our work,' he says. 'For we have much to do.'

* * *

It is quiet outside and the light from the moon shines through the crack in the blinds. I have fallen asleep three times already but something keeps waking me. I tiptoe across the floor and take the Device from its new hiding place – a gap at the back of my desk behind the drawers. Climbing back into bed, I rest it on my lap. The carved letters and shapes glow a soft golden yellow.

'What a clever machine,' I whisper. 'I am able to see you even in the dark.'

My fingers find the grooves and the Device wheezes and sighs, as if complaining that it has been woken from sleep. What will it tell me tonight?

'When?' I whisper.

The pointers shiver and start to move. I hear the *puff, puff, puff* sound and the cogs ticking inside.

Thirty-one minutes past six on the thirteenth of August, two thousand and eighteen, the Device replies.

'Where?'

I work out the distance to be six thousand, one

hundred and sixty-three kilometres.

'That is a very long way from here. In which direction?'

ᚱ ᚗᚏ ᚗᚖ O ᚦ ᚗ

I jump out of bed, grab my computer and sit back on the bed again. There is an 'N' then some numbers and a 'W'. These mean north and west and the numbers are in degrees and minutes. So, looking at my electronic map, six thousand, one hundred and sixty-three kilometres, north fifty-three degrees, fifty-four minutes, west one degree, fifty minutes, brings me to the north of England in the county of West Yorkshire, near to places called 'Thribbleston' and 'Skeldale'. What strange names they have in England.

I place my fingers on the grooves once more.

'Tell me what is going to happen there,' I whisper.

Nothing.

'Hello? Have you fallen asleep?'

I wait, gently tapping its side.

The long pointer begins to edge around the disc. The symbols glow as it passes over them. It looks beautiful in the darkness of my room. The pointer twitches and begins another turn.

'Are you trying to decide something?' I whisper.
It stops suddenly and my body tenses.

I sit up. It takes another turn. Faster this time, stopping on the same symbol.

Again, it turns, and again. I am trembling now.

'No! Please stop! This cannot be true.' Tears are running down my cheeks.

There is a noise from Ma and Da's room. I push the Device under the sheet just as Ma opens the door.

'Are you all right?' she whispers. She comes over and strokes my head. 'Bad dream?'

'Yes, Ma. A bad dream. Very, very bad.'

'You know that dreams are not real.'

But this is not a dream, Ma! I am saying in my head. *It is real! Whatever it means, is certain to happen.* I breathe in deeply and try to sound brave.

'Thank you, Ma. I will go back to sleep now.'

'Call if you need me,' she whispers. 'Goodnight.'

'Goodnight, Ma.'

But I do not sleep.

I cannot sleep.

I may never sleep again until I find a way to warn the people six thousand kilometres away of a catastrophe that is certain to happen.

SEVEN . . .

9

Halo

Jade's come to stay. She turns up at the door at eight in the evening with a suitcase, telling us how evil her mother is and how her dad doesn't care about her.

'Just for a day or so,' Mum whispers to me, as Jade slips off her shoes.

'Can someone bring my case?' Jade asks.

There it is, in the porch. It looks like there's enough stuff for a week.

Dad lifts it inside. 'Goodness me, you've come prepared, haven't you?' he says.

We gather in the kitchen. Mum puts the kettle on and Gran brings out one of her jam sponges.

I corner Mum by the sink. 'Where's she going to sleep?' I whisper.

'We can put the camp bed in your room,' she whispers back.

'It'll be a bit of a squeeze,' I say.

We trudge upstairs with the cake and the bed.

'You put it up,' says Jade. 'I've no idea how it works.'

I sigh. I don't think it's worth arguing. I unfold the camp bed and realise it won't fit. Mum comes up to see how we're doing.

'Let's try moving the bookcase into the corridor,' she says.

My bookcase is in the exact position where I can reach any book whilst I'm lying in bed. I know every story inside out. Every character is alive and living in my head. It's like moving my best friends to the moon.

'Please, Mum,' I say.

I glare at her but she ignores me, so I take the books off the shelf, one by one, and place them carefully in a pile by my bed. She can move the bookcase, but my books are going nowhere.

Jade's staring out of the window, hoping to see Pedro.

'Where is he?' she says.

'Come on, Jade. Give us a hand with the bookcase,' says Mum.

'Oh, I can't, honestly. I'm so tired and, anyway,

I haven't finished my cake.'

Mum breathes out slowly. She does this to show she's slightly annoyed.

'I'd like you to help us,' she says, softly. 'We're making this space for you.'

Jade whips round. 'Sure,' she says, frowning.

The camp bed ends up closer to my bed than I'd like but at least Jade hasn't asked to swap.

Not yet.

I hide in the bathroom and text Pedro.

Clear skies predicted. Star watching at midnight

Cool, comes his reply. **I'll bring hot choc.**

The sky is darkening and the house is still. It feels strange having Jade so close. I can't remember the last time we had a sleepover. We'd be forever having *Harry Potter* marathons, feasting on marshmallows and Jammie Dodgers. Can't remember when we stopped. Or why.

I look over and see her eyes blinking in the half-light.

'Remember that den we built?' she says. 'On the building site. How old were we?'

'Eight, I think.'

'And our dads came looking for us because we were late for tea and they went nuts when they realised half of it was underground and could have collapsed on us at any moment.'

I grin. 'Yeah. That was mad, wasn't it?'

'Yeah,' says Jade. 'Bonkers.'

We laugh for a moment, then there's silence again. I hear Mum and Dad's soft voices in the next room.

'We used to talk about living in a flat together,' she says. 'D'you remember?'

'Yeah,' I say.

'It was going to be in the posh part of Leeds.'

'Is there a posh part of Leeds?'

'Probably. Dunno. I was going to marry that famous cricketer, and you were going to marry that actor bloke off *Emmerdale*.'

'Oh, yeah . . . I *was*!' I don't know how she remembers this stuff. 'Can't understand why, he's awful. Didn't he murder someone in real life?'

Jade giggles. 'Probably,' she says.

I stare through a slit in the curtains. There's one little star twinkling. I wonder how far away it is and how it got there.

'Why do things have to change?' says Jade.

'Just how it is, I suppose.'

'Wish they didn't. Wish everything could stay as it used to be.'

'Freeze time, you mean?'

Jade sighs. 'Yeah, suppose so. So things don't get worse, fall apart . . . you know.'

She heaves in another deep breath and pulls the sheets around her, and we fall quiet again.

It's ten minutes to midnight. Jade's breathing is soft and regular. I shuffle to the bottom of my bed and tiptoe to the bathroom. The central heating clicks into life as if it's warning everyone that I'm on the loose. I take my jumper and jeans, hidden earlier under a stack of towels, and slip them over my pyjamas.

I tread like I'm in a minefield. Down the stairs, gliding close to the wall, straddling the creaky corridor then through the kitchen to the back door.

Pedro's here already, round the side of the house so we can't be seen. We move silently, spreading blankets and setting up the telescope. He's brought a jumper and a woolly hat and two velvet cushions with tassels.

We lie back. The sky is magnificent.

'What will we see tonight?' he whispers.

'Through my Skywatcher telescope, I am going to show you something that will take your breath away.'

It's the Great Globular Cluster. M13. Hundreds of thousands of stars, twenty-five thousand light years away. I settle in my chair and look up.

'Arcturus on my right,' I breathe. 'Vega on my left, then the square of Hercules and along the edge of the keystone shape.' I have goose bumps all over. 'Just look at that,' I say.

Pedro takes my place and nestles in the chair. He sits there, still and silent. The air is cold and, above us, the wind rustles the sycamore leaves.

I crouch near him and whisper, 'The stars we are looking at right now are almost as old as the universe itself.'

Ages later, he leans back and sits for a while. I catch him wiping his face, but I don't think it's just the magnificence of the universe that's making him cry.

He gets up and takes a flask from his bag.

'Hot chocolate,' he whispers.

We slip on jumpers and pull the blankets over our knees.

'So why is Jade staying with you?' he asks. 'I saw her at the window.'

'Oh, yeah. Well, she just turned up. She says it's because her parents are horrible but I reckon it's to see you, really.'

'Me?'

'Yeah. Can't think why, though.'

He grins.

'Tell me about your adventures,' I whisper.

He breathes deeply and closes his eyes.

'Last year, I went wild camping with my dad in the Yukon, Canada. We stayed at an old ramshackle place where we chopped wood and made our own fires and hand-pumped water and hiked up a mountain to see the Northern Lights.'

'That's one of my dreams. What was it like?'

'No words to describe it,' he whispers.

'And the Milky Way?'

'Mind-blowing,' he says. 'Makes you feel very small sitting on our little planet, looking out at the universe.'

A plane rumbles across the sky, its lights flashing in the dark night.

'Where else?' I whisper.

'I learned to follow animal tracks and find water in the Australian outback. That was with Dad as well. There were so many flies buzzing around us, we could hardly see each other's faces. And another time, I went to Zimbabwe where the skies are bigger than anywhere else on Earth and the sunrise is so beautiful it makes you cry. I learned to drive in Africa.'

'*Drive?* How old were you?'

'Ten.'

'But your legs wouldn't have been long enough to reach the pedals!'

'Dad made a few adjustments to the seat and it was a small jeep. No roof, though. We took it out on the dusty roads in the middle of nowhere.'

'No crashing into anyone then?'

'Only a cow.'

'You didn't hurt it, did you?'

'No. Just bumped its backside and it walked away.'

I giggle, then fall silent. As silent as the stars

and the galaxies far above. And I see the sadness in him, the fear, like he's holding it all inside and I want to ask him about his dad and why he isn't here.

'Pedro?' I whisper.

He draws in a breath like he's afraid of what I'm going to ask.

'No, it's nothing.' And I smile at him, blinking in the darkness.

10

Ageze

I do sleep, but only for a few hours. When I wake, all I can think of is that people are going to die and I am the only one who can warn them about it.

People will die if I do nothing.

I cannot get the words out of my head. I sit in the kitchen wondering how I can contact people 6,000 kilometres away. Maybe their priest would listen to me? Or the police? But surely their first question would be, how do you know? And even if I tried to explain that an ancient device has predicted that this will happen on 13 August, would they believe me?

'No, they would not!' I say – out loud.

Ma comes in. 'Are you talking to me?'

'No. Sorry, Ma.'

'Eat your breakfast,' she says. 'You are as skinny as a beanpole.'

'Yes, Ma,' I say.

By the time I have finished eating I have decided that I cannot call the chief of police of Yorkshire or a priest in Skeldale or send an email. No one is going to listen to a twelve-year-old boy from Ethiopia telling them that they must evacuate their village because something terrible is going to happen which will kill people, but he has no idea what it is. And I cannot tell anyone what the Device really does. Not Abdi or the *meri gheta* and definitely not Ma or Da. They would be so angry that I took it from the ground and they would not believe a word about its powers. They would take it to the *meri gheta* and he would lock it up in the museum for another thousand years, and I do not want to think about what would happen in Yorkshire.

The only way is to go to England myself. But how?

We have no uncles or aunts who I could stay with. Not even good friends. I think, hard. What would be the only reason Ma and Da would let me go to England? Maybe doing something to improve myself. I remember Yared's older brother going to a summer school near London. Ma and Da would let me go there, I am sure. I get my computer and start searching. There are many choices – and I find the perfect one in Oxford. This has to be the way to get to England on my own. It has to be.

'Will you be visiting the scribe today?' asks Ma.

'Yes, Ma.'

'Good,' she says. 'Are you making progress with Ge'ez?'

'Yes, Ma. Excellent progress.'

She smiles. As she is in a good mood, maybe this is the time to ask her.

'You know, Ma, I have been thinking about my future. I am very ambitious.'

'Just like your father,' Ma says. 'And that is a good thing.'

'My dream would be to go to university in Great Britain. The very best university. My teacher believes that I will be able to do that. So, I would like to start my preparation as soon as possible.'

Ma turns to look at me.

'You are only twelve years old.'

'Yes, but I must pass my exams with the highest grades. And there are entrance exams and interviews. I do not know if my teacher will be able to coach me to that level.'

Ma thinks for a while.

'What sort of preparations are you thinking of?'

'I would like to go to summer school in England. They prepare students for the universities of Oxford and Cambridge.'

I am not sure this is true but it makes Ma's eyebrows leap towards her hairline.

'It is years before you will go to university,' she says.

'You are a teacher, Ma. You know that a child's education must be built on solid facts and good teaching from the beginning.' I remember Ma saying those exact words and I see a little smile on her lips.

'Da will agree,' I add.

'That is because Da says yes to everything,' she grumbles.

'I would love to go this summer, Ma.'

'You have never travelled outside Ethiopia! Someone would have to come with you and you know that I have your sisters to look after and Da is working day and night on his wind turbines.'

'I am sure it is possible to travel alone, and the summer school bus would pick me up from the airport.'

'I am not sure,' says Ma. She sounds annoyed. She breathes in and out and then says, 'Let me discuss this with your father.'

At least she has not said 'no', so there is still hope.

Back in my room, I take out the Device again. I should give it a name, something to describe its beauty and power. While I am thinking about that, I am itching to put my fingers back on the grooves. Even though it has already predicted the burst water pipe and the terrible event which will soon happen in England, I have a strong urge to try it again. I feel a sense of responsibility.

I turn the key three times and spread my fingers. The symbols glow, even in daylight.

When?

ᚱᚱ ᚲ ᚱᛈᛁᚱ
ᛁᛒ ᚳ

That is today. In half an hour!

Where?

ᛁᛈᛏᚦ
ᚱ ᚦ ᛖ ᛗ ᚳᚱ ᚳᚱ

What?

Fire!

North nine degrees, two minutes. East thirty-eight degrees, forty-five minutes. I work out that the location is just over a kilometre away.

It is the cotton factory next to Abdi's printing works!

I bury the Device in my cupboard, snatch my phone and race outside. Across the skatepark, behind Yared's house, straight down the road, dodging tuk-tuks and taxis, stray dogs and street sellers. I feel everyone's eyes following me.

'What is happening? What are you running from?' someone shouts.

I have no time to answer. In the distance is the red brick wall of the printing works. I charge across the yard, past workers sitting in the shade, to the door of the Fasika Trading cotton factory. Rattles and squeaks from the weaving looms float through the open windows. I stand in the doorway. There are at least twenty wooden looms strung with strands of cotton fibres. One man is making a beautiful weave of coloured threads. Women sit at wooden spinning wheels along the length of one wall. It would only take a spark for everything to go up in flames.

'Excuse me,' I say.

A woman turns and comes to the door. She looks like the boss.

'Who are you?' she asks.

'I have come to warn you that there may be a fire in your factory today.'

Her eyes narrow and her forehead creases.

'A fire? How do you know this?' She tugs me outside to where it is quieter.

I think quickly of an explanation. 'I heard men talking as I was walking through the market. You know there have been a lot of fires started deliberately in Addis recently. I think you should be careful. If a fire starts here, it could burn down your factory.'

'Did your friends make you come here for a joke?'

'No, of course not.' I glance at my phone. It is nearly twelve-thirty. 'I am trying to help you!'

The woman waves her hand. 'Go away, silly boy. You are interrupting my work.'

How ungrateful people are when you are trying to help! I turn and walk away but as I pass the printing works, I have an idea. I put my head around the door. Inside, the printers are shunting and pumping. Workers are concentrating hard. Abdi is on his knees with his hands inside a huge machine.

I run up to him. 'Abdi!'

He smiles.

'Please! I need a fire extinguisher for the cotton factory!'

His eyes widen. 'Is it on fire?'

'Yes . . . it probably is by now. I told the boss lady but she ignored me and people are still inside.'

Abdi points to the wall. 'There! Take it! Go quickly. I will bring another!'

As I race back across the yard, there are shouts and cries from inside the Fasika Trading building. Dark smoke is rising from the factory roof.

I must get up there.

I scramble over a low wall by the doorway then climb up to a higher ledge and swing the canister on to the roof. I pull myself over the gutter and roll on to the tiles. There is already a lot of smoke.

As I cross the shallow roof, factory workers are running out into the yard. Suddenly I am unsteady, terrified that I may fall. The tiles are hot. Even from a few metres away the heat is hard to bear. I think of the fire training we had at school and repeat Miss Bekerie's message in my head, 'If you only remember one thing, it is, do not panic.'

I squat as I pull out the pin of the extinguisher and spray the water jet over the flames, but as I cover one part of the roof, more flames leap up from somewhere else.

Abdi has found a ladder and another extinguisher. He is climbing now.

'It is too hot up here!' I shout.

'Move away,' cries Abdi. 'I will spray the flames. You soak the rest of the roof.'

Black smoke curls around him. I edge back as Abdi opens up another jet of water.

There is a sudden crash. Part of the roof is falling in.

'Move to the end,' shouts Abdi, pointing.

We scramble over the tiles and lie down flat as a great cloud of smoke moves over us.

'Cover your mouth and nose,' he shouts.

I take off my T-shirt and tie it around my face.

'Go down, Ageze,' shouts Abdi. 'It is too dangerous up here. I will follow you soon.'

Flames suddenly burst through another section and one of Abdi's friends climbs up and starts to break open other parts of the roof to let out the smoke.

I watch from the yard below. He drenches the rooftop, quickly stopping the flames on other sections from spreading. All I can see now are patches of broken roof tiles and spirals of thick white smoke.

The workers from the factory come over.

'Thank you, thank you,' they say.

Inside the building, sunlight shines through the holes in the roof and water drips over the fabrics and weaving looms. Abdi is by my side.

'I do not know what to say,' says the Fasika factory boss. She hangs her head and stares at the ground. 'This whole building could have burned down if you had not warned us.' She reaches to shake our hands. 'I cannot thank you enough. You have both been very brave.'

Abdi rests his hand on my shoulder as we walk back to the printing works. He turns and looks me in the eye.

'How did you know there was going to be a fire? It is almost as if you had a warning, a portent.'

I pause. 'It has something to do with the key you

made,' I whisper back, wishing I could tell him the truth. 'That is all I can say for now.'

Abdi pats my shoulder. 'I am very glad that the key has helped, but that does not explain how you knew about the fire.'

'Sometimes strange things happen,' I say, and I smile.

Abdi smiles back. 'You have done well. Take care, Ageze,' he says.

As I make my way to the museum for my appointment with the *meri gheta*, a name for the Device pops into my head.

'A portent,' I say aloud. 'Portend. The Portendo Device!'

There is one window in the room where the *meri gheta* sits – four panes of glass arching over an old doorway. The only sounds are the scritch-scritch-scratch of his pen. Inside a small glass cabinet standing in a dark corner are ancient parchments. Only the *meri gheta* and a few holy men are allowed to touch them. Some are over three thousand years old.

'*Meri Gheta*,' I whisper. 'Could you show me one of these ancient books? I am wondering if they may contain symbols like these.' I show him the paper again on which I have drawn all the symbols from the big disc.

The *meri gheta*'s eyes crinkle. He shuffles to the cabinet and slowly lifts out a rust-brown book.

'This was written by the ancient fathers of the Ethiopian Church. The pages are made of goat skin.'

On the wrinkled yellow parchment, in clear black ink, are the symbols for water and fire, a sword and the sun. Coins and a skull. Exactly as they appear on the Portendo Device.

I point to the coins. 'What do they mean?' I ask.

'Gold,' says the *meri gheta*. 'Wealth and prosperity.'

'And this?'

'It is an eclipse. But also, perhaps, a bad omen.'

'Of course!'

'These swords mean a battle or a fight. Conflict of some sort,' he says.

'And the skull?' I whisper, hoping with all my heart that I was wrong.

'Death,' he breathes.

I feel a tremble through my body.

The *meri gheta* gently closes the book. 'The parchment must not be in the air for too long,' he says. 'We must return it to the cabinet now.'

'Would you allow me to look at it again next time?' I ask.

He glances at me and his lips stretch into a slight smile. 'That may be possible,' he says.

'You smell of smoke,' says Da, sniffing my hair.

It is evening. We are upstairs, watching the sun setting behind the hills.

'I was near a fire. Not that near, just near enough to get smoke in my hair.' I feel my stomach churning. The Portendo Device is turning me into a liar. I quickly change the subject.

'Da, you had a dream once, didn't you?'

'As a boy, I had many dreams,' says Da.

'Was it difficult to persuade Grandma to let you follow your dreams?'

He thinks for a while. 'Yes, I suppose that is true. She did not understand about science and engineering, building bridges and factories.'

'And wind farms,' I add.

Da smiles. 'Your grandma still has no idea how wind farms work.' He laughs.

'I have dreams too, Da. I mean, ambitions.'

'To go to one of the best universities?'

He must have been talking to Ma.

'What do you think?'

'I think the summer school is an excellent idea. You must spread your wings and experience other countries and cultures. It is just a question of persuading your mother.'

I feel a surge of excitement. 'How do we do that?'

'We must work on it together.'

'There is not much time, Da. It could get booked up quickly.'

'I will talk to her. Send me the link so I can read the details and we will all sit down and discuss it together.'

I leap at Da and hug him tight. I feel tears filling my eyes.

'Thank you, Da. I am so excited!'

11

Halo

Twenty past eight on a summer morning. Birds are twittering and the sky is already bright blue. Jade is smiling in her sleep. She looks peaceful for once.

I've been awake for ages. Too much thinking going on. Too many questions buzzing around my head.

An engine hums and a door slams. I shuffle to the end of the bed and tiptoe to the window. There's a big van parked outside Pedro's. A woman comes out of the house in jeans and a T-shirt. It must be his mum. I watch two men lugging boxes up the drive, then a posh settee and a huge dining table. I head downstairs.

'Bit early for you, isn't it?' says Dad.

He's just back from his morning run. He's leaning over the kitchen sink, dripping.

'Couldn't sleep,' I say. 'Did you see the van outside Pedro's?'

'No,' he says.

'They're moving stuff in. Have you talked to her yet?'

'Mrs Ortega? Yeah – said hello a couple of times.'

'Did she say why they moved here?'

Dad looks at me blankly. 'No,' he says.

'She works in a bank.'

'Does she now?'

'You do that sort of stuff – money and things, don't you?'

'Yeah.'

'There's only her, though.'

Dad stares.

'I mean his dad's not there.'

'Ah, I see.'

'But there's Pedro's sister and she's really clever. Going to be a doctor. We should invite them round. They're really nice. Pedro is, anyway.'

'Yeah, we should,' says Dad, but his mind's somewhere else. Probably on spreadsheets or accounts or something.

I make some breakfast and go outside and lie flat out on the grass. This is the best view of the world on a summer morning. Blue sky and tumbling clouds. I listen to the hens scratching around in the hen run and chew on a piece of toast.

Mum's had to buy creamy milk and chocolate cereal for Jade. She won't eat anything else for breakfast. Jade comes down in her dressing gown around nine o'clock, slumps in a chair and starts scrolling through stuff on her phone.

'What are you two doing today?' asks Mum.

'Reading,' I say.

'Sunbathing,' says Jade. 'But first, Halo and me are doing nails.'

I wish I could tell her that I hate nail polish, but she'll probably make a big song and dance about it so I end up choosing 'Moon Shimmer'.

While she plugs in to her latest playlist, I get a text from Pedro.

Can you come to the moor again?

When?

Today. This afternoon

You know Jade's here

I'd rather it was just you

Don't you have to help your mum?

We'll have finished by then

OK, but could be a bit awkward

A few seconds pass.

Just for a while. Meet up in the village somewhere?

OK. See you at the library at 2pm

I find an excuse to leave Jade on her own.

'Mrs Moira Hattersley needs my help,' I say at lunch time, when Gran's weighing out wholemeal flour for the bread maker and Mum's unloading the shopping.

'What's happening at the library?' asks Mum.

'It's the Summer Reading Challenge and Storytime.' This is actually true, it's just that I'm not on the volunteer schedule for today.

'Is it fairy tales?' asks Gran.

'Not today, but I'll take you up there when it is.'

'Smashing,' says Gran.

I'm not proud of making stuff up, telling everyone I'll be in one place when I'm actually going to Pockley Moor with Pedro.

'Will you be long?' asks Jade.

'Don't think so. There's loads of books here to read if you get bored.'

'Are you kidding?'

'I'll find you something to do, Jade,' says Mum.

Pedro doesn't say much. He sets off along Main Street all quiet and serious.

'You OK?' I say.

'Yeah,' he says, but I know he isn't.

The wind hits us hard when we're up on top. We have to lean into it. Streams of grey cloud hurtle along. He wants to go on Grubbit's Scar, the highest point on the moor.

I scan the hills and the splotches of dark trees and lines of pale stone marking the fields. I watch tiny cars edging along the winding roads.

Pedro sits in the tall green bracken and I sit next to him and we listen to the quiet all around us. He keeps sighing and staring into space. I'm wondering if something bad has happened.

There's a spot of rain, then it starts pelting down, huge drops stinging our faces.

'Better get over to the bothy,' I say. 'Quick!'

I grab his hand and we race along the tracks between the heather. By the time we get there our feet are soaked and the grassy paths have turned to mush. The bothy is a shelter for hikers and walkers. We burst in through the door and slam it shut. The only furniture is a table and two scruffy chairs.

Pedro wanders around, looking at a broken mug on the floor and peering at the burnt-out candles above the fireplace. The rain is so loud we can barely hear each other and we sit close so we can talk.

'Don't suppose you've heard of Wiccie's Circle?' I say.

He shakes his head.

'It's thirteen ancient stones and if you step inside and make a wish it'll come true.'

'Who says?'

'My gran. Goes back to the Bronze Age, a thousand BC or something. After that, witches used it for ceremonies.'

'Have you tried it?'

'Yeah.'

'What did you wish for?'

'*The Goblet of Fire* for Christmas.'

'Did you get it?'

'Yeah,' I say.

The rain's blowing horizontally now, battering the metal hut.

'Why did you want to come here?' I ask.

'To get out of the house. My mum's a bit sad. It's difficult seeing her like that.'

He looks sad, too. I'm not sure if I should ask why, so we sit there waiting for the rain to stop, until the sun glints through strips of blue sky.

'D'you want to see the stones then?'

He shrugs. 'OK.'

The stones are worn and gnarled and grey. Some are leaning like they're about to fall. I imagine people dressed in animal furs and huge fires stretching up into the night sky. Haggard old women dancing between them, chanting in the darkness.

'You go clockwise once round the edge, then twice the other way,' I say. 'Then sit in the middle, close your eyes and make a wish.'

He's digging his hands in his pockets. His shoulders are hunched. 'I mean, really . . . ?'

'Come on, it's worth a try. You never know.'

He stands by the tallest stone. He looks at the ground, swings his arms, takes long careful steps.

Three times round, keeping his eyes fixed on the ground, he steps into the circle and sits. The wind drops and the moor falls quiet and still, as if it's holding its breath. Up above, a buzzard glides, tipping and turning under the grey sky. Pedro makes his wish.

And I hope with all my heart that his wish comes true.

SEVEN . . .

12

Ageze

'Have you noticed that your son is going grey?' Ma is standing over me, tugging my hair.

Da comes over to look. 'I would say it is more like silver,' he says.

I have also noticed the silver hairs but when I pull them out, more seem to grow.

'I think you should have a haircut before you go to England,' Ma says.

'But it is the style, Ma. And you know locks take years to grow.'

Ma is not happy with the idea of allowing her eldest child to travel to summer school in a far-away country, on his own. It took many discussions and many promises for her to agree. It was only after Da had talked to the person in charge of the school that Ma finally said 'yes', and the school were happy for me to come after I sent my personal statement and exam grades. Then we all sat down together while I made the booking on my computer.

'You must promise to call or text me every day,' says Ma. 'And what about the flight to London?'

'We will get a visa and he will be accompanied on the flight by a flight attendant,' says Da.

'You have to,' I say, 'if you are only twelve years old.'

'So book the flight now before I change my mind,' says Ma. There are tears in her eyes.

I get up and put my arms around her and say, 'Thank you,' softly, but my stomach is churning because what Ma and Da do not know is that I am not going to summer school at all. And I know I am betraying the people who love me the most but it is for a very good reason. Far away in England, in a small village in Yorkshire, something terrible is going to happen. If I do not go there to warn them, many, many people will die.

It is two weeks before I travel to England. I have been waiting for Ma to leave the house to go to the market. I watch her through the window as she walks into town. I sit at my computer. My fingers are trembling. I know that what I am going to do is very wrong. The problem is that if I do not arrive at the summer school, the staff will definitely contact my parents and I will be in so much trouble, they will make me return to Ethiopia immediately.

So, I have no choice. There is only one thing I can do. I am going to cancel my place without telling Ma and Da.

Dear Madam/Sir

Unfortunately my son, Ageze Tadesse, is unwell and will not be able to attend the Cherwell Summer School. He is very saddened as he was looking forward to a wonderful experience. I must ask you to please cancel his place on the course and the airport transfer bus from Heathrow. Please send any replies about the cancellation to this email address.

My sincere regards,

Sophia Tadesse

I pause for a moment, then click 'Send'.

Oh, Ma and Da, what have I done?

* * *

So here I am at Heathrow airport. The flight attendant who was looking after me has signed me over to someone called Katherine who is taking me through the airport. I have a plastic pochette around my neck with all my documents inside. I have shown my passport and now we are waiting for my suitcase. Is it possible to be fizzing with excitement and trembling with fear at the same time?

'Have you seen it yet?' says Katherine.

She checks that we are at the correct carousel and we watch other passengers lifting their bags from the conveyor belt. I picture the Portendo Device inside my case, hidden in my clothes.

Horrible thoughts stream into my head. What if my suitcase has gone through a scanner and someone has seen it inside? What if it is illegal to bring a unique and ancient device to England and I am questioned and sent back home to be put in prison?

We wait and wait. Almost everyone has claimed their bags. Have they put my suitcase on the wrong flight? Maybe it is on its way to Kathmandu.

'There!' I shout and run to pick it up.

Katherine checks the label and we walk through Customs, where a large man is standing with his arms folded. The Customs man is allowed to stop anyone he likes and search their bags. If he stops me, I could be in big trouble. His eyes follow me as he steps forward.

'Please bring your bag over here,' he says.

I freeze and point at Katherine. 'She has my suitcase,' I say.

'Not you,' he replies, and he nods to the lady behind me.

I quickly follow Katherine through the door in case the Customs man changes his mind.

Here I am stepping into England. I am so happy but my stomach is churning when I think of what I must do now. Somehow, I have to pretend that I am going to the summer school but sneak away and find a train to take me to Leeds.

I see a lady holding a Cherwell Summer School sign. There are two other children near her with their suitcases. Katherine is looking at her watch.

'Over there,' I say. 'Cherwell Summer School. I will be fine now. Thank you for looking after me.' I am hoping that she does not want to come over and talk to anyone but she checks her paper again. 'I have to sign you in,' she says.

'No, no,' I say. 'I will be fine. They know me. I have been going for years.'

'Come on, we have to go together,' says Katherine and she walks across the hall and I follow. I am going to be in big trouble now. I cancelled my place so my name will not be on the list.

The lady holding the sign smiles as we approach.

'Welcome to the Cherwell Summer School. My name's Hannah. What's your name, please?'

I stand next to her, quickly scanning the list that she is holding. I see a name that has not been crossed off yet.

'There, Peter Garnley,' I say, quietly.

She glances at me. 'May I see your acceptance letter and passport, please, Peter?'

I am sure I do not look like Peter Garnley. My heart is banging hard now as I try to think of what to do.

'The letter is in my suitcase,' I say, 'I will find it for you.'

Katherine is calling someone on her phone. She is tapping her foot and looking at her watch. I open my case and move things around slowly.

'Surely all documents are in your pochette?' she

whispers. 'I'll help you look.' She is still holding her phone waiting for someone to answer.

'But I need the letter as well,' I say. 'It is in here. Somewhere.'

I am still not sure how I am going to manage to get away. I pick up piles of clothes and take my time as I place them back one by one.

Katherine looks worried. 'Look, I'm supposed to be meeting another passenger,' she says to Hannah. 'Can I sign to confirm the transfer?'

'I'm sure that will be all right,' says Hannah.

I try not to show how relieved I am and stand up to shake hands with Katherine. 'Thank you for looking after me,' I say.

'Enjoy yourself and have a good time.' And she walks away quickly and disappears around the corner.

'Found your passport, yet?' asks Hannah.

'Still looking,' I say. 'Actually, I really need to visit the bathroom.' I zip up my suitcase.

Hannah sighs. 'No need to take your case with you. I'll look after it,' she says, but I am already wheeling it away.

'Da told me to not to let go of it until I reach

summer school,' I call back. 'I will not be long.'

Hannah hesitates but another student is arriving and she smiles and greets them.

'The toilets are to your right,' she calls after me. 'Come back pronto, the bus will be leaving soon!'

I wheel my suitcase slowly and as soon as I am around the corner, I run. Down the long corridor, swerving past groups of people and bags and trolleys.

Now I must follow my plan.

1: Leave my suitcase in 'Baggage Storage'.

2: Buy food and water for my journey and a ticket for the underground train.

3: Take the underground train to King's Cross station, then a train to Leeds.

I find a quiet corner. I lay my suitcase flat on the floor and look under the layers of clothes. There is the Device wrapped in T-shirts and glowing softly. I put it into my backpack with my phone charger and some extra clothes. Then I take my suitcase to 'Baggage Storage'. It is too heavy to take on the train.

Next, I go into a shop called 'Costa' and take a sandwich from the shelf and a bottle of water.

The queue is long with only one lady serving the customers. The people behind me are muttering about how slow it is.

'Come on, we haven't got all day,' says a man in a hat and a long, rusty beard. He is standing behind. He is breathing beer over me.

When it is my turn, I drop my sandwich. The man groans and clicks his tongue as I pick it up. Quickly, I pull a five-pound note from my wallet, give it to the checkout lady and slip the change into my pocket. I give the rusty beer man an evil stare as I leave.

The underground signs are easy to follow. Before I left home, I found a YouTube video which showed the way through Terminal 3. I walk down a slope then go at super speed along the moving walkway as if I have bionic legs. At the ticket desk, the man gives me a ticket for the underground train and says, 'You won't have to wait long.' He gives me a Tube map so I can follow the stations on the Piccadilly line.

Now, I am really going to Yorkshire. I smile because I am proud of myself but I also feel worried and alone.

At first, there are three people on the train but more and more get on at each station. Soon they are standing very close reading newspapers or books or plugged into their phones. I check the map each time we pass a station. I must be ready to get off at King's Cross.

The doors open and everyone squeezes out. There are so many people on the escalator it feels like my feet are no longer touching the floor. We come out into a huge space and I suddenly feel very small. It is hard to walk in a straight line and I keep moving to the side to let people pass. No one moves to the side for me. I feel like I am invisible.

Through the windows I can see the busy London streets. Everyone is dressed in smart clothes and walking quickly. There is no one carrying parasols or selling carrots and fruits and spices by the roadside. No one polishing shoes on street corners. No blue and white tuk-tuks. I hold the straps of my backpack. How surprised these people would be if they knew what was inside.

I turn back to the station and stand still for some minutes, trying to find the sign to buy train tickets.

My phone beeps.

Have you arrived?

I reply. **Arrived safely in London, Da and Ma!**

Is the air hostess still with you? Are you on the summer school transfer bus? Take care and let us know when you have arrived in Oxford.

Yes, I will, Ma. I am fine.

I switch off my location.

Sorry, Ma and Da, I say in my head.

I always seem to be saying 'sorry'.

I scan the huge departures board. I must be quick. There is a train to Leeds in twenty minutes. I see the ticket office across the hall.

'How much is the next train to Leeds?' I ask the ticket man.

'One way?'

'Yes.'

'Railcard?'

'Yes. No. What is a railcard?'

'No railcard, then. That'll be eighteen fifty, please.'

I open my wallet and search the little pockets. Where are the twenty-pound notes that Da gave me? I feel like I am going to fall. There is only a one pound coin and a folded ten-pound note that Ma must have put in at the last minute. The rest of the money has gone.

'Do you want a ticket or not?' The man is scowling.

'How far can I go with eleven pounds?'

He scans his screen. 'Stevenage,' he says.

'How far is that?'

'About thirty miles.'

'How far is Leeds?'

''Bout two hundred, give or take.'

Even if I caught a train to Stevenage, I would still have one hundred and seventy miles to go. But then I would have no money.

Someone in the queue mutters behind me. 'Hurry up, kid, I've got seven minutes to get to platform three.'

I stand there, frozen. The ticket man asks me to move aside so he can serve the other customers and I shuffle to the door and cross the hall to the exit. How did I lose my money?

All around are busy people and wet buildings and taxis rushing. There is a terrible coldness inside me.

I am alone, Ma and Da, and I do not know what to do.

13

Halo

When I get back, Jade stomps downstairs and bangs the kitchen door open with a handful of clothes and her bulging suitcase. She drops them on the floor. Her eyes look like they could fire laser beams.

'You weren't telling the truth,' she says. 'You're a *pigging* liar, Halo Moon.'

Mum turns round, startled.

'You weren't in the library,' says Jade. 'You weren't doing Summer Reading Challenge and Storytime, were you?'

'Hold on a minute,' says Mum.

But Jade doesn't listen.

'You were on Pockley Moor with Pedro Ortega.' She says his name in a whiny voice.

'Is that right, Halo?' says Mum.

'Well, yes, I was.' I glance over at Jade. 'Pedro asked me, that's why I went. There's something bothering him.'

Jade's eyes soften. 'What's bothering him?'

'I don't know exactly.'

Jade huffs. 'Well, I can go and tell Mrs Hattersley—'

'Mrs *Moira* Hattersley,' I say, interrupting her.

'I'll go and tell Mrs Moira-*flaming*-Hattersley that you're a pigging liar and she shouldn't let you in that library ever again!'

I can see the veins standing out on her neck. She looks just like her dad.

'Look, I'm sorry.' My heart's going a hundred miles an hour.

'You could have asked me to come,' says Jade. 'We've always done everything together.'

'Please sit down, *both* of you,' says Mum. It's not often she uses her firm voice.

I pull out a chair but Jade doesn't move.

'Sit down, Jade, please,' says Mum.

Jade slips on to a seat and glares at both of us.

'Number one,' says Mum. 'No one has the right to address anybody in that manner, Jade. Is that clear?'

Jade shrugs.

'Is that clear?' Mum's voice goes up an octave.

'Yes,' says Jade.

'Number two,' continues Mum. 'You should *never* call someone a liar, especially when you haven't been completely honest yourself.'

Jade sniffs. 'Don't know what you're talking about.'

'In order for you to know that Halo was not in the library, you must have been following her, having told me that you would spend the afternoon upstairs on your computer.'

Jade lowers her gaze, knowing she's been found out.

'Were you?' I say.

'Well, yeah,' says Jade.

Mum looks at me and waits.

'I promised Pedro I wouldn't say anything but if you knew, you'd understand. I didn't want to upset anyone, that's all.'

'See how sneaky she is?' says Jade.

'I was only trying to be a good friend.' I say it slowly, through tight lips.

'But not to me!' She's almost shouting.

Mum sighs.

'Halo, I'm disappointed that you didn't tell us the truth. Please go up to your room while I run Jade home. I think you both need time to cool off.'

'I'm sorry, Jade,' I whisper.

Ten minutes later, the car is back in the driveway. I listen to the creaks as Mum comes upstairs. She knocks and puts her head around the door. She sits on the bed waiting for me to speak.

'Pedro asked me to go to the moor, that's all. He seemed sad about something and he said his mum's sad, too. It was a sort of private thing. I don't think he wanted anyone else to come.'

'I see,' says Mum.

'So, I went with him.'

Mum smiles. 'Well, that was nice of you.'

'So Jade's making a big fuss over nothing, really.'

'Except you didn't tell the truth.'

'There would have been a big fuss if I had.'

'Possibly,' says Mum.

I want to tell her about the longing I saw in his eyes. The despair.

'You should invite them over for dinner or something,' I say.

'Yes,' says Mum. 'That's a lovely idea. I'll do that.'

14

Ageze

It is six o'clock in the morning. The sky is already filled with light. My heart beats fast as I remember where I am. I must have fallen asleep when I was sheltering from the rain. I imagine Ma and Da. They think I am studying chemistry and playing football and making new friends, but here I am sleeping in a car park. I feel shivery and hungry and alone.

I should call them. I should tell them what I have done. They will forgive me and by tomorrow I could be back home and safe again. But what about the people in Thribbleston? I cannot forget about them.

I buy breakfast and as I am chewing on a chocolate pastry, I make an important decision. Today I will turn my back on London and walk north.

Yes, I will walk.

I must.

I have to.

There is no choice.

Google Maps says it is three hundred and twenty-five kilometres to Thribbleston. That seems a long, long way. *Think of it in small parts*, I tell myself. But it is hard to do that and I have to push away the horrible thoughts about losing my way or being kidnapped or running out of food.

One step at a time, Ageze. I take a deep breath. *One step at a time.*

There are big houses along Camden Road, and lines of trees. A red bus rushes along. There are not many people around. Maybe it is too early. I feel the weight of the Device on my back and there is a tingling feeling in my stomach as I imagine the pointers twitching around the discs. I sit down behind a bench and set the beautiful machine on the ground.

'Hello,' I whisper.

I have a warm feeling all over me. Like greeting a friend. I place my fingers on the grooves and wait. But the Device does not show me When, Where, What. Instead, the middle pointer shows north-north-east. And that is all.

'I hope you are not broken.'

I get to my feet and move from left to right and

each time the pointer swivels to the same direction.

'So that is what you are doing! You have found another way to guide me!'

I hold the Device inside my open bag, watching the disc direct me as I walk. My stomach is rumbling. Eating the chocolate pastry seems like years ago.

Not far along Camden Road the Device takes me to a shop selling African food. I stand outside and put my nose to the window. These are all the dishes that Ma makes back home. I cannot believe they are here in a street in London.

A man steps out. 'Hey, bruv, you from round here?'

'No. I come from Ethiopia,' I say.

'Hungry?' I think he can see it in my eyes. He does not wait for a reply. He goes back into the shop and brings *injera* filled with meat and a spicy sauce.

'I am sorry, I cannot pay. I do not have enough . . .'

He pushes it into my hand. 'No need, bruv. It's yours. Enjoy!'

'That is very kind. Thank you! Please, what is your name?'

'Henok. And this here is Lalibela Kitchen. Where you going, bruv?'

'North,' I say.

'Young kid like you, on your own? You sure you're OK?'

'I am fine, thank you. I will have friends there.'

'Good to hear that.' He taps me on the back. 'May God go with you to the north. Take care.'

I am smiling my widest smile. Maybe with my amazing Device and the good people in England, I will get to Thribbleston in time.

Finsbury Park. The Great Cambridge Road. Soon I am crossing a big roundabout over the M25 motorway. The cars are fast and frightening. Google Maps says I have walked twenty-two kilometres. Only twenty-two?

The pavement has gone and I must stay on the grass verge. I try to keep to the side away from the fast traffic but I do not feel safe. Drivers flash their lights as if I should not be here. I keep my eyes on the ground and think only of the people in the Yorkshire village. The next time I look up there are fields all around me.

I am cold and my feet ache. A small shed in the distance looks very welcoming. With heavy legs,

I follow the hedge around the field. The windows are broken but the roof looks solid. I am smiling as I close the door. It is dry in here but cold air is still blowing in, so I hang up my towel to cover the holes in the glass.

Tonight, the moon is bright. I try not to think of bad things. Frightening things. I imagine Ma and Da. What are you doing now? I hope you are thinking of me. Is the moon shining down on you, too?

I text Ma.

Done lots of work today. Busy playing with friends. Love to you all.

Is your bed comfortable? Are they feeding you good food?

Yes, Ma. Everything is fine.

Da says hello and work hard.

I will, Ma. Love to everyone.

I lie down on the wooden floor and think of my family until I fall asleep.

Light shines through the cracks in the door. I sit up suddenly, forgetting for a moment that I am far from home. My stomach growls and my mouth feels like cardboard. I take out the Device and rest my fingers on the base. It shows me today's date, the direction north-north-east and the symbol for wheat.

'Food? That is exactly what I need!'

I jump up, pull on my shoes and slip my bag over my shoulders.

I hold the Device as I walk. It feels safe to do that as I am completely alone, surrounded by fields and hedges and trees. The middle pointer moves this way and that as I make my way towards a road. I follow it as it twists and turns until I see a town in the distance. Before I reach the houses, I tuck the Device back into my bag.

I clean my boots before I go into the supermarket. The lights are bright and when I see my reflection in the glass windows, I can understand why everyone is staring at me. In the toilets, I brush the leaves from my hair, wet a towel and wash my face. The water feels good on my skin.

Back in the shop, I take a basket and fill it with thick sliced bread, orange cheese and water. Even though I look tidier, people are still staring and I am sure that the man in a blue shirt is following me to see if I am going to steal something. I would like to turn around and tell him that I am the son of Dr

Tadesse, who is a pioneer of renewable energy in Ethiopia, and of Sophia Tadesse, a brilliant teacher who volunteers for the orphanage and gives food to the poor. I want to tell this person to leave me alone but he follows me up and down every aisle and is still watching when I pay at the self-service checkout. I wave my ten-pound note at him before I feed it into the slot.

I am an honest boy, I say in my head. *Do not stare at me, Mr Supermarket Man, and judge me from the way I look.*

Around the back of the building there is a quiet place where I can sit and eat. I find a corner out of the wind. I am so hungry it feels like my stomach has scrunched into a tight ball.

'Come on, Ageze,' I tell myself. 'It is time to leave. You must walk at least forty-eight kilometres every day.'

I follow the pointer on the Device as I go. It is taking me on quieter routes, away from the main roads, where there are fewer people to ask questions about an Ethiopian boy walking across England.

'But how do you know that this is the best way to go?'

I wish the Device could answer back. Every time I pick it up I wonder how it knows where I am and the best route to take. What a clever machine!

To keep my legs going, I sing a song that the English teacher taught us at school, all about wandering along a mountain track with a knapsack on my back. The teacher said it was very good for walking. I sing really loud and try to forget how tired my legs are.

By early evening, I have eaten almost half of the bread. Rain is falling so hard it stings my skin. I am wet and cold and shivering. The Device guides me along a narrow road to a church. I stand in the doorway and peep inside. Shadows from the candlelight shiver on the stone walls. I move to a dark corner and sit down.

The Device is back in my bag. I can see it pulsing and glowing.

'Got you this,' says a voice.

A thin girl is holding a towel.

'You're making puddles,' she says.

I get to my feet and take it from her. 'Was I asleep?'

She nods. 'I'm Clara. You can come in the kitchen,

if you like – I'll make a cuppa to warm you up.'

'What is a cuppa?' I follow her through an arched doorway into a kitchen where she is already filling a kettle.

'Cup of tea, silly! You on a walk?' she asks.

'Yes.'

'Where you going?'

I do not want to answer her question, so I say, 'Do you live here?'

'Yes, my dad's the vicar. He's out on visits tonight.'

Clara pours hot water into two cups and stirs in three spoons of sugar. I am still shivering and she brings two more towels, draping one around my shoulders and the other over my head.

'Why is some of your hair silver?' She pulls at little strands and looks at them closely.

'I do not know,' I say.

'My dad would say it's because you're wise. If you were in a fairy tale you would be called Silverlocks.'

I laugh at this. It feels good to be with someone kind and friendly. When we are quiet once more, we sit in the tiny kitchen listening to the rain battering the windows. It reminds me of the storms at home.

'What's that thing in your bag? I saw lights twinkling . . .' says Clara.

'Can you keep a secret?' I say. I am suddenly desperate to share it.

She nods.

'It is a magical machine from an ancient kingdom in Ethiopia.'

Her eyes widen. 'What sort of magic does it do?'

'I will show you, but you must promise not to tell anyone.'

She presses a finger to her lips. 'I won't say a word.'

The Portendo Device glows golden yellow in the gloomy light. Like me, it seems tired and weary. I place my fingers on the grooves and the pointers creep around the discs showing tomorrow's date, fifty-three kilometres north-north-west and a glowing yellow sun.

'What's it doing?' she asks.

'It is telling us that it will be sunny tomorrow and I have a long way to walk.'

'I love that,' says Clara. Her eyes are shining. 'I think you should sleep here. We have a camp bed.'

I am wondering if she might tell the vicar. I must be careful, as I could be sent back home.

'No one will know,' says Clara. 'We don't sleep in the church. We live in the vicarage across the road.'

Later, I hear the door opening and the smell of food makes me sit up.

'Shepherd's pie,' Clara whispers. 'Sneaked a bit of extra gravy on it.'

She sits for a while, watching me eat. 'You didn't say where you're walking to.'

Maybe it is all right if I tell her. It is hard keeping such a big secret inside.

'It is a village called Thribbleston in Yorkshire. I am going there to warn the people of something that is going to happen.'

'Is it something bad?' she says.

'Yes. Watch the news on the thirteenth of August.'

Her eyes widen. 'What are you going there to do? You don't look like someone who does bad things.'

'No,' I say. 'I am going there to save people.'

'That's good, then,' she says. 'Save them from what?'

'I do not know exactly. We will see.'

She gets up. 'I'd better go back. Will I see you in the morning?'

'I do not think so. I must leave early. Thank you for your kindness, Clara.'

'Take care, Silverlocks.'

The door closes and I feel safe and warm and filled with hope.

The next morning, I am awake before five o'clock and find a packet of biscuits. Clara must have put them in my bag. I pull on my hat and keep my head down as I walk, trying not to think of anything. I tell myself to ignore the aching in my legs and the worries in my head. All I need to do is walk.

I travel through towns with strange names that I cannot pronounce. I write them on a piece of paper so I can remember where I have been. I allow myself one biscuit every hour. They are chocolate digestives. The most delicious biscuit in the whole world. As I walk, I sing all the songs that Ma and Da have taught me. I sing them louder and louder as I march along.

At night, after I have rested a short time, I walk to

the nearest town. I find a public house to fill up my water bottle and a plug to charge my phone. I feel ashamed that I am taking food from the bins, but I must eat and I must keep on walking.

SIX . . .

15

Halo

The next morning, I see Pedro sitting at his desk gazing out of the window. He's in exactly the same place as when I first saw him, except I'm not peeping around the curtains this time.

I catch his eye and he stands up and presses his nose to the window.

'What's up?' he mouths.

I do hand signals to ask if I can come over. I point at me, then him, and walk two fingers across my palm. He doesn't get it at first. I mime it again, exaggerating each movement to a ridiculous level. Pedro's laughing so much he falls off his chair. It's lovely to see him laugh. When he appears at the window again, he puts his fingers in the shape of a capital 'T' and I show him a thumbs-up.

I race downstairs and across the road and he's already at the door to let me in. We go up to his room with our steaming cups.

'I didn't use to drink tea,' he says.

'It's normal,' I say. 'Spend any time in Yorkshire and you become an addict.'

He grins.

'You're invited for dinner tonight,' I say. 'Did your mum tell you?'

'Yeah, she was really pleased.'

'It's my mum's birthday today but best not to say anything. She hates people making a fuss. And Norman and his mum and dad are coming.'

'OK,' he says.

My phone beeps.

Need you in the kitchen. Where are you?

'Actually, I'll have to leave the tea. There's a billion desserts to make for tonight.'

'See you later, then,' says Pedro.

'See you.'

And I rush down the stairs and back home to the kitchen.

Mum's birthday is officially at 13:17. We watch the clock and have a countdown.

'What on earth have I been doing for forty-five

years?' she says.

'Being lovely,' says Dad, and he kisses her on the cheek.

Dinner is going to be at seven and Mum's already flapping around like a headless chicken. The table looks gorgeous. I wheeled Gran to the fields earlier to pick poppies and cornflowers and ox-eye daisies. She's arranged them in a vase.

'Do you think they'll like lasagne?' says Mum.

''Course they will,' I say.

'Maybe I should be doing something exotic, like scallops or honey-glazed duck breast.'

'Lasagne's perfect,' I say. 'It's Italian.'

'Do they like Italian?'

'They'll love it, Mum, stop worrying.'

I've been put in charge of desserts. I've already done the apple pie but there's still a blueberry cheesecake and the birthday cake to make.

'It's a lot to do,' I say.

'Ask Norman over to help,' says Gran. 'He loves baking.'

Norman is brilliant with the electric whisk. I sprinkle in the flour while he mixes. When the cake's baked and cooled, I leave him to cover it with chocolate buttons and arrange the candles.

After four hours we're all done. Mum clasps her hands and smiles. 'With all that lot, and Gran's flapjacks, we're going to have a feast.'

It's seven o'clock and we're waiting for everyone to arrive. Norman's clapping and grinning and Mum's peeping around the curtains.

'They're on their way,' she whispers.

She's wearing her one and only dress – bright red with a flower on the shoulder. But she's still got her slippers on and I grab her hand and point to her shoes by the front door. Usually shoes aren't allowed inside but we're ignoring that rule for tonight.

Pedro's mum is called Rose. She's tall and slim with the biggest brown eyes and dimples in her cheeks when she smiles.

'Happy birthday!' she says, as she walks in. She has a sort of American accent.

I glare at Pedro because he wasn't supposed to mention birthdays but Mum doesn't seem to mind so we just giggle and laugh.

'This is our friend, Norman,' I say.

'How doo? How doo? How doo?' shouts Norman.

'Carmela not coming?' I say to Pedro.

He shrugs. 'Didn't want to. Sorry.'

Rose gives Mum a bottle of wine. She goes to Gran and sits beside her.

'I have something for you,' she says. 'An audio book of the world's greatest fairy tales. I heard you like them.'

'How kind,' says Gran. She takes Rose's hand in hers. Her eyes glisten.

Norman's parents, Jean and Pete, arrive with more flowers and it's all drinks and chit-chat for a while. *Where do you come from? What do you do?*

'You'd never believe it, but I was born in Halifax,' says Rose.

'No!' says Mum. 'A proper Yorkshire lass. How lovely.'

'I worked in London, then San Francisco, Zurich, Hong Kong, New York and Dubai. That's where my husband and I met. In a bank.'

'Blimey,' says Dad. 'All over the flipping world, hey?'

'We were all born here and we've stayed put

ever since,' says Mum.

'Same for us,' says Jean.

'Nowt wrong with that,' adds Gran. 'You know where you are with your own folk.'

Rose nods. 'When you've been away for so long you can lose your roots. Forget who you were all those years ago.'

'Is that what brought you back?' says Jean.

Rose looks down. 'In a way,' she says.

There's a lovely smell coming from the kitchen.

Mum gasps. 'Lasagne's ready! Come and help me carry the plates, Norman.'

We gather around the table and Rose admires the wild flowers and says how beautiful it all looks. Pedro and I sit next to Gran.

'So, you're the stargazer in the family?' says Rose.

'Me? Yeah. I love it,' I say.

'Pedro hasn't stopped talking about it,' she says. 'Perseids and comets and delta something-or-others.'

'I think it's important that we know where we're from,' I say. 'Every single bit of this planet was made up there, in the universe.

I think that's amazing.'

Dad and Rose start talking about finance and stock exchanges and trading. And my mind drifts back to Pedro's dad and the stones on the moor.

'Remember Wiccie's Circle, Gran?'

'Oh, aye. Used to go there as a young lass. Made many a wish up there on the moors. How does it go again?'

'*Clockwise once around and twice the other way,*' we chant.

Norman claps.

'Did your wishes come true?' Pedro asks Gran.

'Every single one of them,' she says, smiling.

'They're big stones, Norman,' I explain. 'And you sit in the middle and wish for something.'

'Wish,' he says, softly.

I look at him and draw closer, squeezing his hand. 'I'll take you one day,' I say. 'To Wiccie's Circle. To make a wish. I promise.'

Around eleven o'clock, we walk with Norman and his mum and dad back home. Pedro and I stay outside for a while, heads tipped back, gazing and pointing.

'It's the summer disco at Kirklees tomorrow,' I say. 'Want to go?'

Pedro shrugs. 'Yeah, why not?'

16

Ageze

On day four, after another eleven hours, I am in a small town on the River Trent. It is late in the evening and I need somewhere to sleep. I wait in the shadows outside the toilet building until everyone has gone home. Public toilets seem safer than a park or a shop doorway. I can lock the door and there is a light switch, some soap and a tap. I try to feel grateful that I am lying on a dry floor out of the wind. I fill up my water bottle and thank God for looking after me.

At half past five in the morning, I switch on the light and look around. Today will be my longest walk and for once, my body feels strong. I wash my face and hands and rest the Device on my knees.

'What are you going to tell me?' I whisper.

The pointer on the middle disc shows me the direction I should go.

'You will need to help me today,' I whisper. 'This is going to be a very long walk.'

There is no one in the town. I stride past red-brick houses all joined together in rows. Trucks rush by and soon the pavement disappears and I am surrounded by fields again. For a long time, I walk alongside the river and when I see a sign on a bridge saying 'The Great North Road' I swing my arms and lengthen my stride. *Not far now, Silverlocks! Keep going!*

I am smiling my biggest smile!

Here I am in the city of Doncaster. Everyone is walking so quickly. Where are they all going with their fast feet? People stare straight ahead, too busy to smile, too busy to talk.

Think of good things, I tell myself, *like the six pounds and thirty-two pence in my pocket and that I only have seventy kilometres left to walk on my journey*. But my phone has low battery and I must find somewhere to charge it.

I buy two burgers, eat one and save the other for later.

More and more people are staring at me. *Who is*

this young boy striding through our city? This skinny boy with his head held high and his mud-spattered trousers? I probably smell bad, too. I have not washed properly for days.

I pass a man and his dog sitting on the pavement. His eyes are blank and he is staring into the distance. I have seen faces like this on the streets of Addis. Hungry faces. Faces without hope. I take out my sandwich from yesterday and put it into his hands.

'Peace, brother,' he says. He bites and chews quickly.

'Could you please tell me where I can take a shower?' I ask.

'You're too young to be on the streets, mate,' he says. 'Where y'from? You ain't from round 'ere.'

'I am from Ethiopia.'

'That's a long way!' He laughs and points in the direction of the railway station. 'Try the Wilberforce Centre. They'll let you in. Good on ya', kid.'

The door at the Wilberforce Centre knows that I am here. It slides open when I stand in front of it. Inside, there is a man lying across three chairs. His face is pink and he is snoring. The lady at the reception has tattooed arms and a ring through her nose. The card pinned to her front says her name is Mo'Nique.

'Hello, love. What can I do for ya?'

'I am looking for somewhere to have a shower.'

She frowns. 'What's y'name, love?'

'Yared,' I say. I do not want to tell her who I really am.

'We don't normally have kids in here so young. You in trouble or something?'

'I am not in trouble. I would like to wash myself, if I may.'

She picks up a pen. 'Where d'you live?'

'I do not live in Doncaster.'

She narrows her eyes.

'Where y'from then?'

'I am from Ethiopia.'

She taps her pen on the table.

'You run away from 'ome?'

'No. I have not. I am visiting some friends but I lost my rail ticket and now I have to walk.'

'Where's y'mum and dad?'

I think her questions may get me into trouble. I do not answer.

Mo'Nique's eyebrows squeeze together and she

taps her pen on the desk again.

'What's your surname?' She looks at me as if I have done something wrong. I think I should leave.

'Why do you need my surname?' I ask.

'Just to check you in, love. We take everyone's names when they come in.'

'Diro,' I say. Yared's family name.

'Give me a minute.' She turns and walks into another room.

The sleeping man coughs and opens one eye.

'That's Mo'Nique. She'll be calling the Social,' he growls. He points to a door behind him. 'Get y'self through there. Second door on't left. Get y'self washed then scarper out back.'

I hesitate. I'm not sure what he is saying.

'Go on lad!' he says. He shakes his finger towards the door. 'I'll tell 'er y'changed y'mind.'

I sprint across the reception area and down the corridor. The bathroom door is open and there is a huge shower. There is even a socket in the wall outside the door. I plug in my phone then lock myself inside. Quickly stripping off my clothes, I dive under the hot water. It is the best feeling in the world. I take the bar of soap and scrub everywhere – even my hair. This is the warmest and cleanest I have been for many days. I give my jeans and T-shirt a wash, scrubbing them with soap and rinsing them in the spray.

There are voices outside. I must be quick. I peep into the corridor. My phone has only charged a little, but 32 per cent is better than 25 per cent. Quickly, I dry myself, roll up my wet clothes, pull on my traditional shirt and trousers that I packed for special occasions, unplug my charger and zip up my bag.

I see myself in the mirror. I look like a proper Ethiopian boy now.

Pressing my ear to the door I wait until it is quiet. I must leave without being noticed. I smile to myself. I am becoming an expert at creeping in and out of places.

But when I open the door, I freeze. Mo'Nique is there. Her arms are folded. She is staring at me.

'I am sorry. I will pay for my shower,' I say.

Her serious face changes into a smile. She reaches out and rubs my hair.

'I don't know who you are, love, or where you're going, but here's something to help you on your way.'

She places a sandwich and a bottle of water into my hands.

I am almost crying.

'You take good care of yourself, Yared, and stay out o' trouble. My name's Mo'Nique. Remember that.'

Night comes late here. It is nearly eleven o'clock and the sky is full of angry clouds. The wind blows softly and branches wave against the darkening sky. The birds have different voices that pass from tree to tree through the cool air.

'I am here. I am here,' sings a bird far away.

'I am here, too,' I sing back.

Tonight, I am in a barn in a field. The rain makes music on the metal roof. There are gaps around the doors and the wind is blowing in. I spread my damp shirt and jeans over the straw bales. My boots smell terrible, so I tie the laces together and hang them on the barn door. I hope they will dry by the morning.

I am happy that I have reached this far. I even laugh because there is warm straw all around me and the sounds of animals singing me to sleep.

Another good day, Ma and Da.

**I will make you very proud one day, I promise.
Goodnight.**

I wake with the sun. My legs ache but I feel refreshed. My clothes are not yet dry, so I keep wearing my traditional shirt and trousers. Ma loves me to wear these clothes. I have a robe too, which makes me look very important.

Blue sky and white clouds reflect in big puddles along the farm road. I walk on the grass so my feet do not get wet. I have not gone far when I trip and fall. Something has come loose under my boot. I sit to untie the laces. The sole has almost broken off. How can I walk with only one boot?

With the Device in my hands and treading carefully, I make my way to the next town. It is still early and the streets are quiet. There is a post office and a newsagent, a hotel and a café, but no shops selling shoes.

I do not have enough money to buy shoes, anyway.

A white van is coming along the road. I hide the Device in my bag as the van slows.

'Where're you off to kid?'

'I am walking to Yorkshire,' I say.

'You're already in Yorkshire. What happened to your boots?'

I do not like this man's questions. They make me feel afraid.

'I am not walking to Yorkshire,' I say. 'It was a joke. My father is coming to pick me up. In a few minutes.'

The man's face tells me that he does not believe that.

'I'll run you to the next town, if you like,' he says. 'There's a sports shop. You can get some trainers.'

I do not want to get into a car with someone I do not know.

'That is very kind,' I say, 'but I cannot accept your offer.'

The man nods. 'I get ya. Sensible kid. What size d'you take, anyway?'

'I am sorry but I do not have money to pay for new shoes.'

'That don't matter.' The man gets out and opens the back of his van. He pushes boxes aside and reaches in. He brings out two sandals.

'Here,' he says. 'Reckon these'll fit. And there's

dry socks, too, if you want 'em. Only worn 'em once. Here, kid, take 'em.'

I sit on the side of the road and pull off my wet socks. The man throws me an old T-shirt to dry my feet. The new socks are warm and the sandals fit well.

'Just the job those, aren't they?' He turns and climbs back in the van. 'Take care of yourself, kid,' he shouts from the open window.

'You are very kind! Thank you!'

'Need more good deeds in this world, don't we? Redress the balance, eh?' And he speeds away down the road.

I sit for a while wondering where all this good luck is coming from. I slip open my bag and watch a soft, pulsing glow from the Device.

Twenty-nine kilometres to go. My head is telling me to keep going but my legs are begging me to stop. The pointer on the middle disc is guiding me.

'I am walking to Thribbleston, near Skeldale in Yorkshire,' I say to myself, over and over again.

It is midday and I am on a long, lonely road on a cold, cold hill. I cannot feel my fingers. I cannot feel my toes. Before me are hills and hills and more hills, yellow and rusty brown. I close my eyes and feel the wind on my face. How I miss the African sun.

17

Halo

It's Saturday. Disco night at Kirklees. Pedro and I have been ready for ages but Jade's still faffing about with her hair in the bathroom. She turned up at my house half an hour ago as if we'd never had an argument.

'It's nearly eight,' I say, through the bathroom door.

'Leave me then!' she shouts. 'I'll see you up there.'

I go downstairs to the kitchen.

'You look gorgeous,' Mum says. 'Jade not going?'

'She'll come in a bit,' I say.

'Enjoy yourselves,' says Gran. 'Wish I was twelve again.'

I give her a kiss and a hug, and head outside. Pedro's waiting on the drive and we walk up together.

'Was that Jade shouting?'

'Yeah,' I say. 'She's a bit of a drama queen.'

'A bit?' says Pedro. And he laughs.

It's good to see him laugh.

Music is thumping from Kirklees hall and coloured lights are flashing through the windows. A bunch of kids from Wheeldale and Thornsby are already up to no good – two lads have climbed the drainpipes and are sitting on the roof. Another lot are doing wheelies on their bikes in the car park.

Pedro and me sit on the low wall by the library. Then Jade arrives. She's all done up with lipstick and everything. She strides towards us in a new dress.

'So, what d'you think?' She flicks her hair, spreads her arms and twirls.

'You look lovely,' I say.

'Ready then?' she says. We link arms with Pedro in the middle. 'Come on, you lot. Time for some madness.' And we show our tickets at the door.

Tinie Tempah is blasting through the speakers, making the floor vibrate. It's all lights and lasers and kids bouncing up and down to the beat and hair being flung in all directions. Jade drags Pedro into the crowd. I stand at the side trying to see if there's anyone else I know. I spot Jessy from the chip shop and Ella from the Craven Arms. They look as lost as me and rush over to give me a hug. We huddle and laugh.

It's hard to talk over the noise so we just dance. Rihanna. Little Mix. Beyoncé. I look for Jade and Pedro but they're over the other side near the speakers.

After half an hour, he weaves his way through the crowd. His eyes are wide and he's sweating all over.

'That's it, I'm done,' he says. 'I'm not cut out for discos.'

I fizz with happiness.

'Let's go,' he says.

'Where?'

'Out of here.'

'We'd better tell Jade.'

'I did. Sort of. I said we'd be back at ten thirty to walk home with her. She's dancing with loads of people. She'll be fine.'

He wipes his brow then grabs my hand and

pulls me out of the hall.

We fast-walk down Main Street, legs stretching, bottoms wiggling, trying not to look like we're escaping. It feels like we're getting up to mischief even though we're not, and I'm trying hard not to burst out laughing. Soon we're at the end of the village. Goosecroft Lane.

I glance at my phone. 'Want to see the universe from Pockley Moor?'

'What do you think?' he says.

The lane has no street lights. The lumpy walls and fields have dissolved into a black hollow space. We use our phones to light the road. Cold air wafts around my bare legs. We jog to keep warm and in no time, we're jumping over the stile and heading up the grassy path.

The world is asleep up here and it feels like we're intruding.

We slow down and tread carefully in the darkness, like we're wading through eternity. I'm holding my breath because it seems like something, anything, could fly or leap out at us at any moment.

'This is a good place,' says Pedro.

And we stop and sit.

All is silent. The sky is clear. Cram-packed with stars. We lie back and our eyes are searching all around.

'You can see stars from wherever you are, can't you?' he whispers.

'Pretty much,' I say.

'How is it possible? How can there be more stars than the darkness between them?'

'Tonight, the sky *is* stars,' I breathe.

A cold wind swirls around us. A sheep bleats far away. Things scratch and slither.

'How long is the Wiccie's Circle magic supposed to take?' Pedro whispers.

'Dunno. I'll have to ask Gran.'

'It's just dreaming though, isn't it? They're just a bunch of old stones. Nothing like that can really help.'

'Magic's good when something's happened that you can't do anything about. It gives you a bit of hope.'

Pedro sits up. 'How good are you at keeping secrets?'

'Absolutely excellent,' I say. 'I have a one hundred per cent record for secret-keeping.'

My heart is thumping and my stomach is turning somersaults.

'Are you sure?'

'Yeah, 'course,' I say, softly.

He heaves in a breath and lets it out slowly.

'My dad's in hospital. He's really ill.'

I gasp and clamp a hand to my mouth. I feel like I'm sinking.

'He's in the best hospital for what he has. It's why we moved here. To be closer to him.'

'Oh, Pedro. I'm so sorry.' I wrap my arms around him.

'It happened so fast. Mum can't even talk about it. She told us not to say anything. And Carmela just wants to hide away from everyone. But we can't live like that, can we?'

'I won't tell anyone,' I whisper.

'I know,' he says.

There's nothing more we can say. We just huddle together in the darkness under the stars. It seems like hours later when I check my phone.

'After ten, better get going,' I say.

We wander back to Kirklees and see Jade outside.

She's hugging everyone, screeching with laughter, chucking her shoes in the air.

'Where've you two been?' she says. 'You missed all the fun.'

'Come on, Cinderella,' says Pedro. 'Prince Charming is here to take you home.'

We each carry a shoe and link arms with her down the road. We sing together, take the long way home along Main Street again, past the Spar all dark and shuttered, and the Hotchpotch with its rows of tacky gifts shining in the window. Then soon we're back at Goosecroft Lane heading towards the church. In a mad moment, Jade grabs a shoe and chucks it into the graveyard, then Pedro and her race after it, leaving me alone by the wall.

As the wind drops and the clouds drift apart, a bright moon beams down and I see someone out of the corner of my eye. I turn, and the sight of him takes my breath away.

A boy is walking into our village as if two worlds have just collided – as if the skin of the earth has folded and two points on the planet have somehow joined. His sandals slap the tarmacked pavement. His white robe billows in the breeze. His dark skin glistens in the moonlight. He strides along, head down, past the chippie and the newsagents and the Craven Arms, all grand and regal, like a beautiful prince, heading in the direction of Pockley Moor.

And somehow, in this moment, I know our lives will never be the same again.

FIVE...

18

Halo

We see his hair first. It's glittering in the sunlight. He's nestled deep in the purple heather as if he's been there all night.

We scan the moors stretching for miles all around. There's only us here.

'Who is he?' says Pedro.

'I think I saw him last night when you and Jade were looking for her shoes. He was heading up Moor Lane.'

'You mean he was walking through the village at nearly midnight?'

'Yeah.'

'What's he doing up here then?'

I shrug and stare. 'Dunno. But it'll be all right. We can just say hello and see if he needs any help, can't we?'

His white robe is woven with red and green and gold. As we edge closer, he looks up.

'Hello,' I breathe, and I know that I'm whispering and I want to think it's because of the silence, because we're surrounded by the deep quiet of nature, but really it's because this boy, this stranger, looks like he's walked straight out of a fairy tale.

We stand and watch. We're still being cautious.

'I saw you last night,' I say, 'walking through the village. Are you hungry?' I take out my sandwich box. 'Here. Have them all if you like.'

The boy doesn't wait. He pushes the bread in his mouth and chews fast.

'Lemonade?' I say.

He closes his eyes as he gulps it down. He draws in a deep breath and blows out slowly.

'Thank you, thank you,' he says.

'What are you doing here?' My heart is thumping so much I'm sure he can hear it.

'That is a long story,' says the boy. He glances at his bag where there is something golden, partly hidden by his robe. 'Please sit,' he says.

We settle down next to him and the wind drops and sun beams down on us.

Pedro holds out his hand. 'My name is Pedro.

Pedro Ortega.' They shake and the boy smiles.

'And I'm Halo Moon,' I say.

He looks right into me. 'I am very pleased to meet you, Halo Moon.'

He sips the sugary liquid again and chews the fresh bread and cheese and pickle. His hands and nails are filthy. His feet are scratched and bruised. He gazes blankly, as if he's been hungry for days.

'What's your name?' I ask.

'Silverlocks,' he says.

We see the spirals of silvery hair amongst his black curls.

'Where are you from?' says Pedro.

'Addis Ababa. Ethiopia.'

'Where are you staying?'

'Here,' he says.

I look at his bag. There doesn't seem room for a tent. In any case, camping isn't allowed on the moors.

'I needed to see this place.' He gestures to the scrubby grass and heather and the rolling hills beyond. His voice drifts into the wind. 'I think we will have time.'

'Time for what?' says Pedro.

But Silverlocks says nothing.

'Are you in some sort of trouble?' I say.

Silverlocks shakes his head. 'I am very tired.'

'You can't stay up here,' says Pedro. 'Come with us to the village. You can rest at my house.'

We head back along the road. Pedro gives Silverlocks a piggy-back when he can't walk any more. Mrs Clegg spots us and comes to the door of the newsagents. Irene trots around from the chippie.

'Ooo, you look exhausted, love. Wait right there!' she says.

'Who's this, then?' says Mrs Clegg. 'Are you all right?'

'He's visiting,' I say. 'And he's fine, just a bit worn out.'

Irene comes back with a bag of chips. 'Here you go. Get those down you.'

I realise the news of Silverlocks will spread around Thribbleston in no time, so Pedro's house seems the best place to let him rest for a bit. He makes a space for Silverlocks on the settee then goes to the kitchen.

'What did he mean, "I think we'll have time"?'
I whisper.

Pedro shrugs. 'I suppose he'll tell us when he's ready, but he probably needs to eat and sleep first.'

He makes hot chocolate and I heat up the chips. We take them through and sit quietly as Silverlocks munches and slurps.

'Thank you for inviting me to your house,' he says.

'You can stay until you're strong enough to go back home,' says Pedro.

Silverlocks stares at the floor. 'That is very kind, thank you. Can you tell me how many people live in this village?'

'About four hundred,' I say.

'How far is the next village?'

'Five miles – give or take. It's called Skeldale.'

Silverlocks nods. 'This is what I thought.'

I want to ask him why he walked here. He sees me looking at his feet again.

'I walked two hundred and two miles,' he says.

'Two hundred!'

'Where from?' asks Pedro.

'London.'

'Just to see the Yorkshire moors?' I say.

'I wanted to take a train but I lost my money.'

A car door bangs and Carmela walks in carrying shopping bags.

Pedro jumps up. 'Just a minute,' he says. He leaves the room, pulling the glass door closed behind him.

Carmela puts down the bags. She's glancing at Silverlocks and me through the glass. I watch them whispering.

I hear Pedro's voice. 'He's exhausted . . . we don't know why . . . he needs to rest . . . she's not going anywhere, she's my *friend*.'

Carmela throws her arms in the air and Pedro comes back in, closing the door behind him.

'Maybe I should go,' I whisper.

'No,' he says. 'She's not really angry. Just a bit stressed.'

Silverlocks is lying down now, with his bag tucked underneath him. Pedro covers him with a blanket and we watch his eyes flutter and close as he slips into sleep.

'Pedro?'

'Come on,' he whispers. 'Follow me.'

We go up to his room. He sinks into a bean bag, elbows resting on the bed behind him. I sit on the chair by his desk.

'Did you see the golden thing in his bag?' I say.

He nods.

'What d'you think it is?'

'He's keeping it close, so something important.'

'And the silver in his hair, how can it sparkle like that?'

Pedro shakes his head. 'I don't know,' he says.

'Will your mum be OK about him staying here?'

'I think so. Anyway, she's hardly around at the moment.'

My phone buzzes. Mum's sent some rubbish with asterisks and hyphens. I think it's meant to say, 'Where are you?'

I reply.

Please use reading glasses when texting

'Lunch time,' I say to Pedro. 'Better go.'

'Come back later, though, won't you?' he says.

''Course,' I say.

* * *

Jean, Norman's mum, calls around after lunch. I overhear her chatting to Mum.

'Who's the mysterious stranger, then?' she says.

'We don't know yet,' says Mum.

'Your Halo and that new lad'll know more. They were the ones bringing him off the moor. I saw them out of the window. Half-dead he looked. God knows what he's been through, poor soul.'

'Well, let's not jump to conclusions,' says Mum. 'Wait while he's had a rest.'

'Is he staying here, then?'

'No,' says Mum. 'Pedro and his sister have taken him in. I think Mrs Ortega is travelling again.'

'Someone should contact his parents. Or Social Services,' says Jean, under her breath.

Mum pats Jean's hand. 'Let him recover a bit first. We don't even know his proper name yet.'

'You should ask Dr Shah to take a look at him.'

'Now that is a very good idea, Jean. I'll call him right away.'

Dr Shah pops over later that evening. Mum and I go with him to Pedro's but we all leave the room while he does the examination.

'A little bruised and battered but basically sound,' says Dr Shah, when we're allowed back in again. 'Some good Yorkshire food will see him as right as rain.'

'I can help with that,' says Mum. 'I mean, I know Pedro and his sister can look after themselves but an extra shepherd's pie and a few apple crumbles here and there won't do any harm, will they?'

'And we'll need to call his parents,' whispers Dr Shah. 'Find out why he's here.'

'Of course,' says Mum. 'Leave that with me.'

As the doctor heads off home and Mum trots back over the road, Pedro helps Silverlocks up the stairs into the spare room. We make up the bed and he flops down, not even bothering to pull the covers over himself. I notice he's wearing a beaded necklace with a little key and wonder what it's for. His breathing softens. His bag is by his side, with his arm across it and the top unzipped. I can just see the golden object inside. Pedro and I glance at each other and have a silent conversation.

Should we?

I'm not sure.

He's asleep, he won't know.

But it doesn't seem right, does it?

Just a peep?

Pedro leans over and holds open one side of the bag. We see the edge of it, the tiny engravings and strange symbols.

What is it? I mouth.

Pedro shrugs and shakes his head.

We peer further in.

'It's incredible,' I whisper. 'There's discs and pointers.'

Silverlocks shifts suddenly and we pull back. I put a finger to my lips and point to the landing and we creep along to Pedro's room.

'What the heck is it?' I say.

'Could be an astrolabe, or some sort of compass. Maybe he used it to find his way here.'

'It looks more complicated than a compass. You don't think he's stolen it, do you, from a museum or something?'

'That would be daring and very difficult.'

I look at Pedro and I can't stop grinning.

'A mysterious stranger with a golden disc turning up in Thribbleston – I can't believe it.'

19

Silverlocks

I open my eyes. The sun is shining through the curtains and I am in Pedro's house, lying on a soft bed. I feel around for the Device. Here it is, safe by my side.

I think of Ma and send her a text.

Hello. Busy day today. I will be learning about robotics then we will play Quidditch! I will make you proud of me, Ma and Da, I promise. I miss you all

One day they will understand why I am doing this.

There is a knock on the door and a whisper: 'Are you awake?'

'Please come in,' I say.

It is Pedro.

'How are you?' he says.

'I am not as tired as before, but I am aching everywhere.'

'It'll wear off soon,' says Pedro. He gives me a

bottle of water and I drink and drink. 'Come down when you're ready,' he says. 'There's beans on toast.'

'Thank you,' I say.

I move slowly across the room. I think of why I came to this village in Yorkshire and my heart fills with dread.

I am standing at the top of the stairs with my bag over my shoulder when the doorbell rings. It is Halo Moon. She takes off her shoes and looks up at me. Her eyes shine when she smiles.

'I've brought fresh eggs for breakfast,' she says.

Pedro cooks, then puts everything on the kitchen table.

'Have as much as you want,' he says.

I eat quickly. I seem to be taking everything. Halo makes more toast.

'Mum wants to contact your parents,' she says. 'Do they know where you are?'

'They know that I am in England,' I say.

'But do they know you're here, in Yorkshire?' asks Pedro.

'They think I am on a three-week summer school in Oxford. But I cancelled it.'

'Why?' asks Halo.

'Please, wait a moment,' I say. I stand up and bring my bag. 'In my country, there are many treasures that are buried beneath the ground. I found this near a church.'

I lift out the golden device and place it in front of them.

'What on earth?' says Halo.

Pedro stares and stares. He leans over and studies the patterns and symbols and the inscriptions. They both look at the cogs at the back and feel the shapes engraved in the metal. Their eyes are wide with wonder.

'What is it?' asks Halo. 'What's it for?'

'It was made in the ancient Aksumite kingdom in the north of Ethiopia,' I say. 'It is more than two thousand years old.'

'Two thousand!' Halo stares.

'What docs it do?' says Pedro.

'Things you would not believe,' I whispcr.

'Tell us,' says Halo.

'I have called it the Portendo Device,' I say. 'It predicts the future.'

'No! Really? I mean . . . it's not possible!'

Pedro is staring at me, now. I think he is trying to

work out if I am telling the truth.

'You're serious, aren't you?' he says.

I nod.

'Show us, then,' he says. 'Show us how it works.'

I remove my necklace and take the little key. I wind up the Device and tell them how I put the pieces together, how it gives a date and a time, a place and a symbol to show what will happen.

'The numbers and letters are written in Ge'ez,' I tell them. 'A very old language from my country.'

'How many times have you tried it?' says Halo.

'A few.'

'How far in the future does it go?'

'I do not know.'

'What happened the first time?' asks Pedro.

'It told me that there would be water, fifteen metres from my house, at seventeen minutes past one.'

'And was there?'

'Yes,' I say. 'A pipe burst and two boys were trapped in the flood and my friend, Yared, and I rescued them.'

'That must have been scary,' says Halo.

Pedro is scowling. I do not think he believes me.

'And it happened at that exact time, fifteen metres from your house?'

'Yes,' I say.

'And the second time?' asks Halo.

'It predicted a fire in a factory. I was there in time to warn the owner but she did not listen. With the help of my good friend Abdi and another workman we put out the fire ourselves.'

'You were very brave,' says Halo.

'Can anyone use it?' asks Pedro.

'I am not sure,' I say, 'but I think it makes predictions that the person using it can do something about, or it helps them in some way.'

'If that's true . . .' says Halo slowly, '. . . and it's not that I don't believe you, it's just that it's so difficult to think that anything can really, truly predict the future – but, if it *is* true, this machine is completely and utterly awesome.' She brings her feet up on to her chair and hugs her knees. 'It was a prediction that brought you here, wasn't it?'

'Yes,' I say.

'Something about Pockley Moor?'

'Yes.'

'What is it?' she says. 'What's going to happen?'

I see the fear in her eyes. I look down at the floor.

'Something bad?' she says, softly.

'It has told me that many people could die.'

She gasps and covers her mouth.

'No,' says Pedro.

'But only if we do nothing,' I add, quickly. 'We have time to warn everyone so that no one will be hurt.'

'But it hasn't told you exactly what it is?' says Pedro.

'No,' I say.

'Are you sure? Have you tried it again?' says Halo.

'Many times,' I say. 'It is as if that part of the warning will come from somewhere else. Someone else.'

20

Halo

The Device sits on the kitchen table. Pedro leans back and folds his arms and, after a while, I realise he's staring at me, as if I'm supposed to know what he's thinking. I glance at Silverlocks. He's doing the same. I feel my face reddening.

'What?' I say. 'What is it?'

Moments later, I get it.

'*Me?* Why *me?* I mean, that's stupid, why should *I* know?'

'Because you're the link,' says Pedro. 'You're the one who saw Silverlocks arrive here. You're the one who knows Pockley Moor. You're the one who knows this place and people better than anyone.'

'That doesn't mean I know what's going to happen.'

'The Device will show you,' says Silverlocks.

'I don't want to,' I say. 'I don't want to be the

one who shows how people in my village could die.'

'You must,' he says. 'It may be the only way that we can save them.'

Pedro puts his arm around me. 'Sorry, Halo. At least try and see what happens.'

'Place your fingers here,' says Silverlocks.

I perch on the edge of my chair and spread my fingers over the slots. Not quite touching. Not quite ready yet.

'I don't want to do this,' I whisper.

I look at Pedro and he presses his lips together into a sort of smile. Silverlocks stares hopefully and I think of how brave he has been to come all the way from Ethiopia and walk across the country to warn us. I have to be brave, too.

I lower my fingers and touch the metal. A pointer twitches and my hands jump up.

'Stay calm,' says Silverlocks. 'It will not hurt you.'

I touch the grooves again and the pointer starts to edge around the disc. There's a little puffing sound from inside.

'What's it doing?' I say.

'The pointer on the smallest disc moves first,' says Silverlocks, 'to give the date.'

We watch it stop and start again as Silverlocks translates the Ge'ez symbols into numbers.

ጋ፫ ፰ ፰ጀ፲፰

'This is the date that it gave me. Thirteenth of August, two thousand and eighteen,' he says.

The pointer moves again.

፮ ፴፩

'What does that mean?'

'Thirty-one minutes past six in the morning. It is the time when it will happen.'

The pointer on the middle disc shifts slowly, clockwise.

'Now the distance from where we are and the direction,' says Silverlocks.

My hands are less shaky now but my head is still trying to make sense of what this machine is doing. I am placing my hands on it and it's telling me the future. How can this be happening?

The pointer stops and starts. Again, Silverlocks translates the symbols.

፰ጀ፱

ደ ፱፫ ፱፰ Ი ፩ ፱

Pedro punches the coordinates into his phone.

'Just over two kilometres from here . . .' he says. 'It's Pockley Moor.'

Now for the prediction that we've been waiting for. Silverlocks's breathing quickens. Pedro leans forward nervously, rubbing his hands on his jeans.

As I place my fingers over the grooves again, something happens that none of us expects.

All the symbols on the large disc, that seemed to be fixed into the metal, push themselves outwards and, one by one, sink back inside the disc leaving a circle of empty spaces.

I snatch my hands away. 'Holy moly! Did I do that?'

'I think so,' whispers Silverlocks. 'Although this has never happened before. Put your fingers back.'

I touch the Device again and we hear a faint ticking and whirring from inside. Three or four seconds pass, then there's a click and a buzzing noise and a new symbol appears. Another one emerges. And another, until all the slots are filled.

Silverlocks stares.

'What's it doing now?' says Pedro, his eyes wide.

The large pointer edges its way around the disc, then stops. My heart is beating so fast I can hear it in my ears.

'A star?' says Pedro.

'With a tail,' says Silverlocks. 'A shooting star.'

'It's a meteor,' I whisper. 'The light when a meteorite falls to earth. And if it's big enough, there's a sonic boom – a shock wave – that can bring down anything in its path. On the thirteenth of August, it's a meteorite that's going to fall on Pockley Moor.'

FOUR . . .

21

Halo

Sometimes I wish I were at Point Nemo.

It's the place on Earth that's the furthest away from any land. I'd be in a little boat with a canopy and a book, just rocking on the sea. I could stay there for days if I wanted to. I'd have a storage box packed with dried fruits, crackers and vitamin C tablets, and a machine that makes fresh water out of sea water. And masses and masses of books.

Some days I'd just drift and doze. I'd close my eyes and think of all the stories about the ocean like *Moby Dick* and *Treasure Island* and *Earthsea*. Other days I'd talk to the porpoises and whales and feed the fish.

But most of the time, I'd be reading.

Another name for Point Nemo is the 'Oceanic Pole of Inaccessibility' – which sounds perfect if you've just found out that a meteorite's going to fall near your village and all you want to do is run away.

But right now, I'm back home at 5 Halley Road checking on Gran, when I'm supposed to be going to Pedro's to decide what we should do, but someone is walking up our drive.

The doorbell rings. It's Mr Ackroyd and I'm in an immediate state of Red Alert. Number one on our List of House Rules is: *'Don't let Mr Ackroyd in.'* Dad's got this technique where as soon as he sees it's Mr Ackroyd, he holds the front door with one hand, barges through the gap and pulls the door closed behind him. He gets stuck outside for a while but it's better than having Mr Ackroyd inside. But Dad's not here right now, and Mr Ackroyd has already seen me, so I'm obliged to go downstairs and open the door.

I'm peeping through a five-centimetre gap.

'Dad's not here,' I say.

'What about y'mother?'

'She's not in, either.'

'When's y'dad back?'

'Not for ages, possibly a century.'

He doesn't take the hint. His face is beetroot

and he keeps tugging at his moustache.

'I'll wait then,' he says.

'I'll tell him you called,' I say.

Mr Ackroyd looks at his watch. 'No, no, I prefer to wait. *Inside.*'

I open the door wider and pretend to be gazing at something across the road. I'm still hoping Pedro will appear so I can put on my terrified face and he'll come and help.

There's no sign of him.

'It's only me and Gran,' I say. 'And Gran's in the toilet. She's been there for quite a long time and will need some assistance very shortly. Probably right now, actually.'

She's not, but I'm hoping that will put him off.

'I'll come in for a bit then,' he says. 'I've something very pressing.'

'Mr Ackroyd?' I say, quickly. 'The thing is . . .' but I can't think of anything and he's already shouldering the door and stepping inside.

'. . . would you mind leaving your wellies on the mat?'

Number two on our List of House Rules is: '*Ask visitors to take off shoes.*'

Mr Ackroyd shakes off his wellies in the porch and marches down the hall, straight into the kitchen, where he sees Gran isn't on the toilet but is making flapjacks.

'Afternoon, Aida. Any chance of a cuppa, love?'

He hasn't even sat down yet.

Gran gives him a wave and I put the kettle on.

'How do you like your tea?' I say.

This is an important question, as number three on our List of House Rules is: '*Ask visitors what sort of tea they prefer (even if you don't like them).*'

I added the last bit.

'So you can stand a spoon in it,' says Mr Ackroyd.

'Strong, then,' I say.

'Better make it a pot. I might be here for a while.'

Not if I have anything to do with it, I say in my head.

'Sugar?'

Mr Ackroyd holds up his hand and spreads his fingers.

'*Five?*' I say.

He nods and I enjoy imagining him with no teeth.

'Milk?'

He nods again.

'Tea bag in or out?'

He rolls his eyes as if it's a stupid question. But it isn't. People can be very fussy about their tea bags.

Mr Ackroyd still hasn't sat down, but that's not unusual. He likes to pace when he's having one of his rants.

'We have,' he starts, 'a stranger in our midst.'

My heart thumps.

'Who has arrived in our village . . . *un-in-vited*.'

'Who's that, then?' says Gran.

'A young gentleman from *foreign* parts.' He says 'foreign' like it has a bad taste.

'That's nice,' I say. 'Like the Brits in Spain.'

'I don't think he's here on his holidays,' says Mr Ackroyd.

'How d'you know?' I say.

'He's not staying in a hotel.'

'Have you checked all the hotels?'

Mr Ackroyd's eyes say he's about to shout, but I don't care. Somewhere in my head I'm making a note that this is the first time in my life I actually hate someone.

'Maybe he's camping,' I say.

'*Stealing* things, more like,' says Mr Ackroyd.

'But he only arrived two nights ago.' I'm definitely sounding cross now.

'Take it from me, things have been going missing very recently.'

'Like what?' I say.

Mr Ackroyd takes a notebook from his inside pocket. He licks a finger and turns a page.

'One barbecue fork. Mr Taylor. Two pegs from Mrs Thwaite's washing line. One windscreen wiper from outside the village hall. A patio pot complete with eight red geraniums. The Prestons' cat.'

'The Prestons don't have a cat,' I say.

'As I said,' says Mr Ackroyd, 'it's one of the items that's gone missing.'

'*Really, Mr Ackroyd!*' I'm about to explode when I hear the front door opening.

'Barry,' says Dad from the corridor. He marches into the kitchen and they shake hands. 'Saw your wellies. How's it going?'

Gran and me escape to the front room with the flapjack. Gran's shaking her head.

'I don't like that man. I *really* don't like him.'

I can't say anything because I'm about to burst with crossness. In fact, I have never felt so cross about anything.

How can you look at someone and know who they are or what they're like?

How can you know someone's story without letting them tell it?

Silverlocks has come here to save us!

'It just isn't right!' I'm shouting now, hoping Mr Ackroyd can hear me. 'What he's saying JUST ISN'T RIGHT!'

'Couldn't agree more,' says Gran.

I text Pedro.

OK to come over?

Yeah, he texts back.

'Let's go to the moor,' I say. I've barely stepped through the door. I'm trembling all over and my heart is pounding.

Silverlocks rests his hands on my shoulders and his dark eyes stare right into me. 'Are you all right?'

I shake my head. 'No. I'm absolutely not all right. I have to see the moor.'

'Now?' says Pedro.

'Immediately,' I say.

We hurry up Moor Road. Pedro keeps glancing at me, expecting me to say something. Silverlocks walks, head down, arms swinging, moving in silence until we reach the top.

'Here,' I say.

We're at the place where we first saw him. Our Ethiopian boy with silver in his hair and a smile like sunshine. The boy who walked two hundred miles to save us.

The sky is so blue, it's hard to believe that beyond are a zillion stars and planets and galaxies, and that we're sitting on a tiny, rocky marble in amongst all that vastness. So alone and so vulnerable.

'I needed to see where it's going to happen,' I say. 'You know, to make it real. I can't believe it's going to fall here, that it's going to burst through the atmosphere and crash right where we are now.'

Tears spill. Pedro covers his face and Silverlocks sits, head bowed in silence.

'We can't let it destroy all this,' I say. 'High

Crag and Ingilby Foss and the grouse and the heather. And our village. You know there are shock waves when a meteor strikes? Remember the one in Russia? The whole of Thribbleston could be in ruins.'

'We can't stop a meteor,' says Pedro, softly.

'But broken windows can be mended, can't they?' I say. 'Walls can be rebuilt. And the heather will grow again and the grouse and the skylarks and the adders will come back, won't they? Tell me that will happen.'

Silverlocks just stares, and Pedro shakes his head slowly.

'I hope so. I really hope so,' he says.

'And you know the worst thing?' I say. 'No one's going to believe us because you can't predict meteors. I'm so scared that no one's going to listen. And you came all this way, Silverlocks. You walked all this way and no one's going to believe us.'

Tears trickle down my face.

We reach out to each other and join hands as the wind rushes around us and the silvery grass shivers and sways.

'We're all going to think of something we can do,' says Pedro. 'No more talking until then, OK?'

'OK,' we say.

Pedro and Silverlocks busily scroll through stuff on their phones. I just sit there thinking and staring at the sky. It's me who breaks the silence.

'We should at least try to warn *someone*. Even if they say it's impossible to know a meteor's coming. What about the Center for Near Earth Object Studies, or NASA?'

'Or the International Astronomical Union?' says Silverlocks. 'Look, here is a list of all the asteroids coming close to the Earth. We should go through them to see if it is on there.'

He passes his phone and we scan the website, but it's too complicated and we can't make sense of it.

'Come on! Think! We have to do *something*,' I say.

Eventually I summon up the courage to call Leeds University. I speak to one of the lecturers who knows about near earth objects.

'This is not a prank,' I say to him.

He's very polite but says it's extremely difficult

to predict meteors and if I see one I should report it to the International Meteor Organisation.

'I *know* it's difficult,' I say, when I've hung up. 'It's only objects bigger than a kilometre they can detect, and not all of those, either.' I sigh. 'It's up to us, then. How are we going to get everyone to leave?'

'There is only one way that I can think of,' says Silverlocks. 'Who are the leaders? Who does everyone listen to?'

'Doctor Shah,' I say.

'Then we must show him the Device.'

'Do you think that'll be enough?' I say.

'What do you mean?' says Silverlocks.

'If we're going to convince him that it can predict things, he may want to try it himself.'

'And the villagers?' says Pedro. 'Will they all want to try it, too?'

I shrug. 'I don't know.'

'The Portendo Device is very powerful,' says Silverlocks. His voice is quiet now. 'If many people know about it, maybe one of them will want to take it and use it for bad things.'

'Then we'll show Dr Shah first,' I say, 'and if we

have to, the villagers as well. But as soon as you're back home you'll have to bury it again. Then you'll be the only one who knows where it is.'

22

Silverlocks

It is four o'clock in the afternoon and we are all in Dr Shah's office. Everything is neatly placed on his desk. He brings more chairs and asks us to sit down.

'We've chosen you because we know you'll listen,' says Halo. 'At least, you'll take what we're going to say seriously.'

Dr Shah nods slowly. I wish he would smile.

'Silverlocks would like to tell you the real reason he came to Thribbleston.' She glances at me, then back at Dr Shah.

I take the Portendo Device out of my bag and place it on his desk. Dr Shah leans forward and puts on his glasses. We watch his eyes narrow and his brow furrow as he looks at the lines and engravings, following them with his fingers. I am not sure if he is angry or surprised.

'What an extraordinary object,' he says. 'What is the script?'

'Ge'ez,' I say. 'The ancient language of my country, Ethiopia.'

Dr Shah touches one of the discs. The pointer shivers but I do not think he notices. He looks in his desk drawer and takes out a little torch and shines it over the inscriptions.

'Quite incredible,' he breathes. He sits back and clasps his hands. 'How did you come across it?'

'I found it in the north of my country, buried on a hillside near a church.'

'Do you know what it's for?'

'Yes. It predicts things.'

'Predicts?'

We all nod.

'What does it . . . predict?'

'I tried it first in Addis. It predicted a burst water main and a fire.'

Dr Shah's eyes widen. I do not think he believes me.

'This time, it's something more serious,' adds Halo.

I look at Pedro. He just stares back.

'I am very sorry to tell you, Dr Shah, but the Device has predicted that on the thirteenth of August, a meteorite will fall on Pockley Moor, large enough to kill many people.'

The doctor stays perfectly still and looks at each of us. Halo reaches for my hand. She is trembling and her eyes are filling with tears. Dr Shah sits back in his chair and presses his fingers together.

'A meteorite?' he says. 'As far as I am aware, meteorites cannot be predicted.'

'We know that,' says Halo. 'We thought the same as you. But it did.'

'I am a man of science,' says the doctor. 'I apply the scientific method. Observe, describe, suggest an explanation, then use that explanation to predict the results of new observations.'

'Then please observe the Device for yourself,' I say.

'Observe it, describe it . . . then let's see about the explanation later,' adds Pedro.

Dr Shah sighs and glances at his watch. I really hope he is not angry.

'What do I have to do?' he says.

'Please rest your fingers on the grooves,' I say.

We gather behind him as he re-examines the inscriptions and the engravings. Then the doctor moves forward in his chair. He spreads his fingers and the moment he touches the Device the smallest pointer twitches and his hands jump into the air.

'How on earth . . . ?' he says. He stands up and peers around the back. I think he is looking for wires.

'We do not know, exactly,' I say.

'To be honest, we have no idea at all,' whispers Halo.

Dr Shah sits down again and puts his fingers back on the Device.

'If it has something to tell us, the Device will give six numbers first,' I say. 'I will write them down for you.'

The Device follows its ancient pattern. The smallest disc – When. The middle disc – Where.

'It's moving much faster this time,' whispers Halo.

As the pointers stop and start again, I explain what each symbol means.

'The date is today and the time is now.' I give Pedro the coordinates and he finds the location on his phone.

'Somewhere on Cold Edge Lane,' he says.

'Please keep your fingers in position,' I say to Dr Shah, 'and it will tell us what the prediction is.'

The last time we used the Device, the pointer on the largest disc moved slowly around the symbols as if it was thinking about which one to choose. But this time, it moves directly to the symbol of a skull, which makes us all gasp.

Even Dr Shah.

'Death,' I whisper. 'We need to go straight away.'

'Now wait a minute,' says Dr Shah.

'We don't have a minute,' says Halo. 'Please, Dr Shah! Come on!'

Dr Shah grabs his medical bag and we race outside and down a lane behind the houses.

I lead the way, following the swing of the arrow on the middle disc with Halo and Pedro close behind as we hurry along. The wind is strong and rain is falling hard, like a tropical storm.

'Follow Silverlocks!' shouts Halo.

I run fast, grasping the Device with both hands like a steering wheel. It keeps pointing to one house in a long row of houses.

'Here!' I shout.

'It's Mrs Midgley's,' says Halo. 'Our school dinner lady.'

Dr Shah runs up the steps and tries the door.

He bangs on the window.

'Someone try the back door,' he yells.

Pedro races around the side of the house and seconds later, he is opening the front door and Dr Shah is inside kneeling by a lady who has collapsed in the hallway. He calls for an ambulance.

We stay outside until the ambulance arrives with flashing lights and sirens and Mrs Midgley is taken away on a stretcher with a mask over her nose and mouth.

Dr Shah watches from the front steps.

'She'll be all right,' he says. 'But it was close. Come on, all of you. Come back with me to the surgery.'

Dr Shah brings us all cocoa and a towel. He switches on the heating.

'Warming up now?' he asks.

'Yes, thank you,' we say.

He stares out of the window looking serious. I think he is realising the power of the Device and that what I told him is true.

'This is a lot to take in,' he says. 'And to be honest, it's completely thrown me. Now we have the real possibility of a meteorite falling on the moor.'

'It's not just a possibility,' says Halo.

'May I see the Device again?' he asks.

I place it on the table and Dr Shah moves closer, studying the largest disc. He runs his fingers around the edge. 'Where is the symbol for a meteor?'

'There are more symbols,' I say. 'Inside.'

'Inside?'

'We only discovered them yesterday, when Halo used the Device,' says Pedro. 'Try it again, Halo.'

It is starting to get dark now and Dr Shah gets up to switch on the light. I turn the little key in the back and Halo presses her fingers on the base. We all watch as the new symbols appear.

'Extraordinary,' says the doctor.

'There it is,' she says, pointing.

'Indeed,' says Dr Shah. He sits for a while, thinking. 'The experience with Mrs Midgley shows that this Device can predict events – one event, at least. If a meteorite does fall on the moor the main danger will be the shock wave after it strikes the ground. It could blow in windows, even bring down buildings. You were right to ask for help. However improbable this may seem, we cannot ignore this warning. We must take action.'

Pedro's eyes are shining and I am smiling my widest smile. Halo puts her arms around Dr Shah.

'Thank you,' she says. 'I knew you'd believe us. I knew it.'

'One last thing.' Dr Shah turns to Silverlocks. 'Did you come all this way just to warn us of this?'

'Yes,' says Silverlocks.

'You are a very courageous young man and I thank you. Something concerns me though – do your parents know where you are?'

'They think I am studying at summer school in Oxford. But I have been texting them every day. Look.' He shows the doctor the messages on his phone.

'Did you arrange to study here so you could come to Thribbleston?'

'Yes,' says Silverlocks.

The doctor gives a little smile. 'Call them and let them know you're all right,' he says.

'Yes, Dr Shah. I will.'

23

Halo

'Come here a minute,' says Mum. She touches my forehead. 'No fever.' She presses down on my chin and peers into my throat. 'Looks all right, so what's the matter?'

'Nothing,' I say.

'It's not nothing, Halo. I can see something's wrong.'

'It's nothing, Mum. Really.'

I'm back home. We only found out about the meteor this morning and even though we've talked to Dr Shah, the worry has been building inside. I'm bursting to tell Mum and Dad but maybe it would be better if they heard about it at the village meeting.

'Must be tired or something,' I say. 'How's Gran?'

'She's fine. Taking her usual nap.'

'Where's Dad?'

Mum frowns. 'Where he always is. Upstairs, in his office.'

'I'll take him a cup of tea, then.'

Mum puts her hands on my shoulders and looks into me. 'If something's happened, it's best you tell someone.'

'Yes, Mum,' I say.

'I'm always here if you need me.'

'I know that, and thanks.'

'By the way, how's the new boy doing? Did you find out his name, yet?'

'No – just Silverlocks.'

Mum grins. 'Straight out of a fairy tale, eh? Wait till I tell Gran. Has he told you why he's here?'

'Sort of,' I say.

'I'll have a chat with him later so we can contact his family and tell them he's safe.'

'No need. Dr Shah's done that already. The chat, I mean. Silverlocks has been sending his mum and dad texts and he's going to call them soon.'

'Right,' says Mum. 'And you're sure Dr Shah's actually spoken to him?'

'Yes, I was there.'

'Very good, then,' says Mum.

I take Dad a big mug of tea, then whizz over to Pedro's again.

24

Silverlocks

We are sleeping outside tonight. Me and Pedro and Halo. We lie on the grass staring up at the night.

'The stars, the constellations, the galaxies, seem eternal,' says Halo. 'Fixed in space. Always here. Like anchors.'

We put up a tent to keep out the cool breeze. Halo brings her telescope.

'Saturn,' she says. 'You can see its rings.'

This is the first time that I have looked at the sky like this. Suddenly I am so close and it feels much more real. I stare and stare, blinking in the darkness.

'The rings are made of ice and rock,' whispers Halo. 'Some are as small as grains of sand and some are as big as houses.'

She shows me Jupiter and its four moons. We find Cassiopeia. The more we look, the more stars there are. I suddenly feel small and afraid sitting here on this little planet, when I know a piece of fiery rock is rushing towards us.

There is a sudden flash.

'What was that?' I whisper.

'The Perseids,' whispers Halo.

'All the burning dust and ice from the comet Swift-Tuttle,' says Pedro.

Halo smiles.

We lie down in the tent with our heads on our pillows and gaze upwards. We follow the strips of silver streaking through the night.

'Is it starting?' I whisper.

'Maybe.'

'We are not going to die, are we?'

'I don't know,' says Halo.

'I feel afraid.'

'Me, too,' says Pedro.

'What can we do?'

'Nothing,' says Halo. 'Except to be as far away from Pockley Moor as possible.'

It is one o'clock in the morning. Complete silence. I glance over at my new friends.

'Are you asleep?' I whisper.

'No,' whispers Pedro.

'I can't stop thinking about it,' says Halo. Her eyes shine in the darkness.

'I cannot, either,' I say.

Halo sits up. 'I don't know why, but I'd feel happier if we were inside.'

'I would too,' I say.

'Let's go then,' says Pedro. 'We can crash out in the sitting room. Just don't wake Carmela.'

It is five o'clock now. Nearly dawn. Even inside the house I could not sleep. I have come to sit in Pedro's garden on the soft green grass.

Da and Ma will be awake now. They will be talking in the kitchen and making coffee. They will be laughing together as they always do.

I call Da.

'Ageze! Is that you?'

'Da!'

'How are you? How are you? It must be very early in England. Why are you awake at this time?'

'I woke up and I thought of you and Ma.' There are tears in my eyes. I want to be there, safe at home with my family.

'It is so good to hear you,' says Da.

'Is there something wrong?' It is Ma's voice. 'Let me talk to him . . . hello! Hello!'

'It is me, Ma.'

'You sound quiet. Has something happened?'

'No, I said I would call you. I am missing you and Da.'

'We miss you, too. You know, you will be coming back soon. It is not long now. You must have made many friends over there.'

'Yes. Some very good friends. Everyone is kind.'

'Have you been warm?'

I think of the rain soaking through my clothes and the cold wind on top of the hills.

'Most of the time,' I say.

'Your sisters are missing you. They were asking why you have not sent them pictures.'

'Tell them that we will have a picture show when I am back home.'

Ma laughs. 'They will be very excited.'

We are quiet for a moment.

'May I speak to Da again?'

I hear Da's deep voice: 'Hello.'

'Da, I need to know something. Please do not be

worried, but I was thinking if anything happened here, would you come and bring me home?'

There is a long pause and my heart is beating fast.

'Da?'

'Ageze, why are you asking this?'

'There is nothing wrong, Da. I am happy here. I am asking because it would make me feel safer, that is all.'

'Of course, of course, I would come. You know I would travel around the world three times for my beautiful son.'

My eyes overflow and tears run down my face.

'Thank you, Da.'

The phone crackles and it is Ma's voice again.

'Has anything happened, Ageze?'

'No, Ma. I needed to be reassured. I feel a long way from you.'

'Of course. It is normal. You know what I have been wondering?'

'What is that, Ma?'

'Are you changing your underwear regularly?'

I smile. 'Yes, Ma. We even do our own laundry here.'

'Really?' Ma laughs and laughs. 'Then you can

continue that when you are back home.'

'Are you sure? OK, I will try. I will see you both soon.'

'Goodbye!' says Da. 'Stay safe and warm!'

'Goodbye!' I say.

THREE . . .

25

Halo

I'm still at Pedro's the next morning when the doorbell rings.

I see her hair and suntan through the glass. I sigh and open the door.

'Heard another lad's turned up,' she says.

'Yeah,' I say.

'Walked from London, or something.'

'That's right.'

'Who is he?'

'He's called Silverlocks.'

She pulls a face. 'What sort of a name's that? Is he here?'

'Yes,' I say.

Jade walks in like she owns the place. There's no time to hide the Device. It's there on the floor by the fireplace.

'Hello, you,' she says, prodding Pedro's chest.

Silverlocks is on the settee eating chocolate cereal.

'I'm Jade,' she says. 'Halo said you walked here.'

'I walked from London,' he says.

'Why?'

'I did not have money.'

'But why did you come *here*?'

Silverlocks is about to say something when Jade spots the Device. She goes over and kneels to touch it.

'What the heck's this?' She tries to turn the discs. 'What's it for?'

'Be careful,' says Silverlocks. He moves fast and takes it from her, gently.

'It's lighting up!' says Jade. 'Did I do that?'

'I will take it upstairs,' says Silverlocks.

'I'm not going to break it,' says Jade.

'It is very valuable.'

'You afraid I'm going to nick it, is that it?' She turns and scowls at me. 'What have you been telling them about me?'

'Nothing!' I say.

Silverlocks settles back on the settee. 'Please sit here,' he says to Jade, patting the space beside him.

'Don't,' I say to Silverlocks. 'Think of what it's told us already.'

'It has helped to protect people,' he says.

Jade sighs and gets to her feet. 'Always so serious, Halo.' She comes over and sits next to Silverlocks. She nudges him. 'Go on then, show me,' she says.

'Place your fingers here.'

Jade touches the base and giggles and grins. 'What's going to happen?'

'It tells the future,' says Silverlocks.

She snatches her hands away. 'You're kidding me.'

'It is true,' says Silverlocks.

'Nah,' says Jade. She looks at me and Pedro. 'Does it? Does it really?'

Her eyes shine brightly. We gather around. My heart's banging. I'm terrified it's going to be something bad.

'You don't have to do this,' I say to her.

'Yeah, actually, I do.'

'It's not a game. It *will* tell you the truth.'

'You're just scared it's going to say I'll be a top model and have seven kids and live in an enormous mansion.' Jade spreads her fingers over the grooves. Her smile has gone now and there's darkness in her eyes. 'Go on then, magic man. I'm ready. Show me my destiny.'

Silverlocks reads the date and time. 'The first of September, two thousand and eighteen at nine o'clock.'

'Oo! That's soon!' says Jade.

Now the middle disc. I find the location on my phone.

'St Hilda's Road, Nottingham,' I say.

Jade leans over to look. 'Where's that?'

'The Midlands.'

'What's the Midlands got to do with me?'

'Keep your fingers in place,' says Silverlocks.

The pointer on the largest disc swings. We're all leaning over to see where it stops.

Jade moves closer. 'What are those?'

'They are scrolls,' says Silverlocks.

Jade shrieks. 'What a load of old rubbish! At the beginning of September, I'm going to Nottingham to get some scrolls!' She rocks on the settee, giggling.

'Scrolls represent learning,' says Silverlocks. 'Studying.'

I've zoomed in on the map now. 'St Hilda's is a school,' I say. 'A boarding school.'

* * *

I walk back with Jade. We don't speak for ages. We usually cross at the corner to avoid Rex, the crazy Alsatian, but we just let him bark at us this time. We're almost at her house and we haven't said a word.

'I mean, really,' she says. 'A stupid thing like that can't tell your future. Nothing can.'

I stay quiet. I don't know what to say. We walk a few more steps when she turns suddenly and grabs my shoulders.

'Oh, my God, it can, can't it? I mean, they told me I was going to a new school but they never said it was so far away.'

Now her brow's all crinkled and tears are trickling down her cheeks. I throw my arms around her and she grabs me back.

'Oh, Halo, what am I going to do?' she squeaks. 'What am I going to *do*?'

26

Halo

Dr Shah stands at the front of the village hall. We're sitting at the side – Pedro, Silverlocks and me – watching everyone arrive. Usually you can only fit about eighty people in here, but Mrs Moira Hattersley has been in charge of seating arrangements and has miraculously made space for a hundred and fifty.

I lean over to Pedro and whisper, 'Where's your mum?'

'Visiting Dad again.'

'And Carmela?'

'She's there, too.'

'Thanks so much for staying,' I say.

I help Miss Finch to a chair and say 'Hello' to Mr Gubbins. The Thackreys and the Howeths, with six in each family, take up a whole row. Jade is the last to arrive, with her mum and dad. She comes to sit with us while her parents slump at the back with their arms folded, as if it's already a waste of time.

'It's true about the school,' she whispers.

'Oh, no,' I say.

'My dad's going to live in Italy and they're going to sell the house.'

'Oh, Jade.' I wrap my arms around her and hold her tight.

'We'll message every day though, won't we?'

''Course we will,' I say.

'And you'll send me stuff to make me smile? Latest gossip and everything?'

Tears are filling my eyes. 'Yeah, 'course I will.'

On a small table near us, the most valuable and amazing object in the world is covered in my flowery pillow case.

Dr Shah clears his throat. 'Residents of Thribbleston,' he starts. 'Thank you all for coming here this evening. During my time as a doctor, I have had to deliver good and bad news. Bad news, of course, is never easy. The news I have to announce this evening is easily the strangest and the most unexpected of all.'

Eyes widen. Heads turn. There are a few whispers and mutters.

'I would like to reassure you,' he continues, 'that what I am about to tell you is absolutely true. It is genuine and has scientific evidence behind it. In other words, it is beyond question. Nevertheless, it will come as a shock to each and every one of you.'

'Quick-quick! Quick-quick!' shouts Norman.

'Thank you, Norman,' says Dr Shah. 'I will get to the point. This brave young man' – he turns and gestures to Silverlocks – 'came here to warn us of a catastrophe.'

Someone gasps and the muttering grows louder. Dr Shah continues.

'Halo and Pedro helped us understand what exactly that catastrophe will be. We now know, with certainty, that on the thirteenth of August, in six days' time' – he pauses to take a breath – 'a *meteor* will fall on Pockley Moor.'

There is absolute silence. Until Irene Siddle pipes up.

'Oh, for goodness' sake!'

Mrs Clegg follows. 'A meteor? What are you

talking about?'

'Is this a joke?' shouts Donald Spud.

Then everyone joins in.

'Please,' says Dr Shah. He waves down the noise. 'If we can all be quiet for a moment, we will explain to you how we know.' He clears his throat. I can see he's nervous, which makes me feel worse. 'This is not a hoax or a dreadful joke,' continues Dr Shah. 'There will be a meteor strike on that day. We don't know how big. We don't know the damage it may cause. What we are sure of is that there is nothing we can do but get out of its way.'

Mrs Clegg raises her hand. 'But they's not the sort of things you know are coming, are they?'

'You are correct, Mrs Clegg, but we do have proof. Absolute proof that this will happen.'

'Come on!' shouts Donald Spud. 'No one can predict them things. What is this?'

Dr Shah shakes his head. 'If you can all be quiet, we will show you.'

'Whatever it is, it's his fault,' says Mr Ackroyd, jabbing a finger at Silverlocks. 'He's brought nowt but trouble to our community from the moment he arrived.'

I stride over to Dr Shah and grab the microphone.

'*Mr Ackroyd!*' My voice comes out louder than I thought possible and I am immensely pleased. 'Someone needs to tell you that you have no idea what you're talking about! You don't even know Silverlocks. You haven't even spoken to him.'

Mr Ackroyd's face reddens.

'What is it going to take for you to realise that Silverlocks has come here to try to save our lives?' I'm talking like the politicians do on TV, using my hands to emphasise everything. 'This twelve-year-old boy has travelled from *Ethiopia*. He has *walked* across England to warn us that this is going to happen! To warn YOU, Mr Ackroyd!'

There's a low rumbling of agreement.

Dr Shah stands up and gestures for Pedro and Silverlocks to join us. He takes back the microphone and scans the worried faces.

'I know it's difficult for us to understand how such a catastrophic event could happen here, but we must take this warning seriously. The day before the predicted strike, we *must* collect up our most precious belongings and transport ourselves and our livestock, and spend a few days in Skeldale.

We must cordon off the roads to prevent anyone returning to Thribbleston. The moor, of course, will be completely off limits.'

A little boy puts his hand in the air. His mum tells him to stand on his chair.

'Yes?' says Dr Shah.

'Can I bring my hamster?' he says.

Dr Shah smiles. 'We must bring all our pets with us,' he says.

'Excuse me! Excuse me!' Mrs Midgley is at the side of the hall, in a wheelchair, waving. Pedro passes her the microphone.

'I know this news is a shock to everyone.' Her voice is croaky and she gives a little cough. 'And I know that what they're telling us is hard to believe, but without this young lad, I wouldn't be here.' She stretches her hand out to Silverlocks and he walks over to take it. 'For those of you who haven't heard yet, this young lad told Dr Shah I was poorly – don't ask me how he knew, but he did – and they all came rushing round to my house and got me to hospital in time. Without these youngsters' – she pauses to wipe her eyes – 'without these young people, I wouldn't be here.'

There's a round of applause. Mrs Moira Hattersley raises a finger.

'May I ask a question?' she says. 'Silverlocks, how did you know Mrs Midgley was ill?'

'Yeah, good question,' says Mr Ackroyd. 'How *did* you know?'

Silverlocks stands up, walks to the small table and pulls the pillow case off the Portendo Device.

'What the heck's that?' says someone.

'A clock or something.'

'What, with three discs?'

'Stolen property, more like,' shouts Mr Ackroyd.

'No,' says Silverlocks, forcefully. 'This is the Portendo Device. It comes from my country, Ethiopia. I found it in pieces, buried near a church. I fixed it together and made it work. At first, I did not know what it was for. But now I know that it tells the future.'

No one moves. No one utters a word.

'Mr Ackroyd,' says Silverlocks. 'Please come to the front.'

All heads turn to Barry. He fidgets a bit and scratches his bald spot, then shuffles along the row and walks up the aisle.

'Please sit here,' says Silverlocks, 'and put your fingers, gently, on these grooves.'

There's a deadly hush in the room. Some people stand up so they can see better.

When the pointer on the small disc moves, I note down the numbers as Silverlocks translates them.

'It's predicting something that will happen today,' I say, loud enough for everyone to hear. 'And it has given us a time.'

Pedro glances at his phone. 'Three minutes from now,' he tells everyone.

'About five metres from here,' I say. 'Just outside the door.'

The symbols on the large disc start to sink inside the Device.

'What the heck's going on now?' says Mr Ackroyd.

'It must be choosing a new one,' I say.

Silverlocks nods.

More villagers are standing up and a few at the back are balancing on their chairs. Others make their way along the aisles to the front so they can see. Mrs Moira Hattersley moves in, her glasses balanced on the end of her nose. Dr Shah is whispering 'Extraordinary' over and over again. Then Mum and Dad come to look. Everyone is watching as the new symbols appear, one by one, in the empty spaces.

The pointer clicks, swings, then stops.

'Snow?' says Pedro.

'Too big,' I say.

'Ice snow,' says Silverlocks.

'I think you mean hail,' says Mr Ackroyd. 'Looks like hail to me.' He gets to his feet, pushes out his chest and clears his throat. 'So, ladies and gentlemen of Thribbleston. Today, the seventh of August two thousand and eighteen, five metres from where we are now, this thing 'ere' – he jabs a finger at the device – 'tells us there's going to be a hail storm. Can you believe it? A flipping hail storm, in the middle of August! Anyone brought a brolly?'

The room fills with laughter. Some of the villagers stand up and wander outside looking up at the blue sky. A few seem to be heading back home.

'Is the meeting over, Dr Shah?' asks Irene.

'Well, no,' says Dr Shah, and he's about to say something else when his voice is drowned by a crack of thunder. The sky darkens. Heads turn and ears tune into a slow *pit-pat*, *pit-pit-pat* on the roof.

One by one, people get up to take a look through the windows. Those outside run back in as the pattering quickens.

'Well, I never!' says Irene.

'Would you look at that!' says Mrs Midgley.

Huge white blobs are falling, bouncing off the grass, clattering over the roof.

Mr Ackroyd stares outside. 'You've got to be joking,' he says. 'It works, that machine of yours. It flipping works!'

I feel Pedro squeezing my shoulder. Silverlocks is next to me smiling his widest smile. Dr Shah shakes his head in disbelief.

'Well done,' he says to us. 'Very well done indeed.' He claps to get everyone's attention again. 'One last word, please.'

The noise subsides.

'I think we have demonstrated, without

question, that this device is able to make accurate predictions. So now we must prepare for the meteor. As soon as we can, we will provide leaflets explaining what each and every household must do during the evacuation. One final and very important request. Some of you may have already realised that in the wrong hands this device could do a lot of harm. So, please *do not* talk to anyone else about it. Thank you for your attention and your time.'

There's a lot of chatter as people make their way out of the hall.

'What's going to happen to the village, then?' asks Irene.

'There'll be an enormous hole on the moor,' says Mr Ackroyd.

'Depends how big the meteor is,' says Donald Spud.

'Let's hope and pray it's just a little one,' says Mrs Moira Hattersley.

We stay behind for a while so Silverlocks can tell his story to Mum, Dad and Gran. When we get to the part about my prediction of the meteor, they just shake their heads, hardly able to believe any of it.

'It is true,' says Silverlocks. 'Halo made the new set of symbols appear for the first time. She must have connected with the device in a different way.'

Mum wraps her arms round me. 'Why did you keep all this to yourselves? I knew something was wrong. You should have told us.'

'We weren't sure if anyone would believe us,' I say.

Dad stands up and rubs his hands together. 'Right. Despite this being the most incredible thing I've ever heard in my life, we have a lot to do, so we'd better get cracking. We need a plan and we need to start getting organised.'

'Indeed,' says Dr Shah. 'The sooner, the better.'

27

Halo

On the day of the evacuation, we're up at five o'clock. I'm in charge of the list and making sure everyone follows it. Leaflets explaining what they have to do have already been delivered to all the residents. Cows, sheep and horses have been moved to fields around Skeldale in the days before. Today, it's people and pets.

We go with Dad, starting at one end of the village and working our way to the other side, house by house, street by street. Some families leave in their own cars. Dad drives the van to take those who don't have their own transport, plus all the bits and pieces that everyone can't bear to leave behind.

Around nine o'clock, Jean Fitchett rushes down her drive clutching two plastic bags.

'I'm sure we've forgotten something,' she says.

Norman is biting his thumb and taking lots of

tiny steps in a circle. 'Blithering heck! Blithering heck! Blithering heck!' he keeps shouting.

'He's getting stressed,' says Jean. 'He'll be better once he's moving.'

When we reach Jade's house, their new red Range Rover Sport is at the end of the drive. Jade's dad, Trevor, is packing suitcases into the boot. Jade and her mum are waiting in the car.

'Need a hand?' shouts Dad.

'No, thanks,' Trevor shouts back. 'Can almost see out now.' He tries the boot door again but it bounces open. 'Shift that flaming vanity bag!' he yells. He bangs it down once more and this time it closes.

'There may not be room for all that in Skeldale town hall,' says Dad.

'Oh, we're not going there,' says Trevor. 'I've booked us in at the hotel for a few days, over at Rookwith Hall. We can all get a bit of pampering until this mayhem blows over.'

He waves and as he jumps back in the car, he says, 'By the way, are we insured for flaming meteors?'

He doesn't wait for an answer. The Range Rover

Sport backs out of the drive and is about to leave when the rear door flies open and Jade leaps out with her bag. She runs towards us and bangs on the window.

'Let me in!'

I push open the door and she scrambles inside next to Norman.

'I'm coming with you,' she says.

'What the hell are you doing?' yells her dad.

'I'm staying to help,' Jade yells back.

Her mum shouts, 'Jade! Come back! I'm not leaving you in the path of a meteorite.'

Trevor is climbing out of the car and striding over. There are thick creases across his brow. 'Do as your mother says,' he shouts.

'No,' says Jade. 'I think it's more important to stay and help. Not run away.'

We watch Trevor's face grow redder as if he's about to explode. 'Do as I say. You're coming with us.'

'We're the only ones *not* going to Skeldale and I don't think that's fair.' Jade stares at her dad for a few moments then grabs my hand. She's trembling.

Trevor turns to Dad.

'Will she be all right with you?'

'Of course she will,' says Dad.

Trevor looks back at Jade and wags a finger. 'Behave yourself, then. We'll be back in a couple of days.'

He walks to the car, revs the engine and speeds away up the road.

Dad heaves in a deep breath. 'Right. Back to business. Who's next on the list?'

When all the occupants, dogs, cats, hamsters and valuables from each house are on their way to Skeldale, Jade sticks a green 'tick' on their front window meaning 'this house has been evacuated'.

It's the older people that are the most difficult. They want to bring everything with them. Tins crammed with old photographs, boxes full of new photographs, mementos from times gone by. Supermarket bags stuffed with tablets and ointments, creams and vitamins. Many of them have tears running down their cheeks as they turn to wave goodbye to their homes.

You can understand why. The whole of

Thribbleston could be blown to bits by tomorrow.

The Skeldale mayor is there to meet everyone. The town hall has been kitted out with extra tables and chairs. Blankets and mattresses are piled up in a room at the back. There doesn't seem nearly enough for all of us.

Backwards and forwards we go. Mum and Dad are allocated to the town hall and families with young children are in Skeldale library. This is the best place for them because of Story Time Corner and the play park outside. We're going to sleep here as well, with all the other kids who can look after themselves. Mrs Fitchett is staying, with Norman.

'Will you help me keep an eye on him?' she says. 'I'm a bit worried about him being in a new place. He doesn't like change, see. I mean, he usually sleeps through but he might get confused in such a big space and it would be a comfort to know you're looking out for him.'

'I'll watch out for him,' I say.

Gran's also staying in the library so she can use the lovely disabled toilet and whizz up and down the slopes and around the bookshelves.

Of course, Mrs Moira Hattersley immediately puts herself in charge, even though it isn't her library.

'There will be fairy tales after tea,' she announces.

'Could we have my favourite, *Sleeping Beauty*?' says Gran.

'I'm sure we can,' says Mrs Moira Hattersley, 'and bedtime stories for the little ones at seven,' she adds. She's already sticking up notices to remind everyone.

'Can I help with the stories?' asks Jade.

I look at her. I can't believe she's volunteering.

'That would be marvellous,' says Mrs Moira Hattersley. 'Come with me now and we'll sort out some suitable books.'

As we're about to head back again to Thribbleston to pick up the next load, Mrs Fitchett runs out and knocks on the van window.

'Norman's forgotten his cuddly toy,' she says. 'Please pop into my house and fetch it for him. It's a rabbit. On the table, next to his bed. He'll fall to bits when he realises he doesn't have it. You won't forget, will you?'

All day long, we work our way across the village, following family cars and tractors, carrying the most valuable items, sleeping bags, duvets and pillows, down to Skeldale.

I overhear Dr Shah and Dad talking to the mayor outside the town hall.

'As we discussed,' says Dr Shah, 'we have very good reasons to believe that the meteor will fall somewhere on Pockley Moor. The village is cordoned off and no one should be anywhere near there until the all-clear is given.'

The mayor mumbles, 'To be honest, this sounds like a load of old nonsense to me, but if there's any chance of people getting hurt we're happy to help. What time will you be putting up the road blocks?'

'Eight o'clock this evening,' says Dad.

By half past seven there are only six of us left in the village – me and Pedro, Silverlocks and Norman, Dad and Dr Shah. Norman ended up coming in the van with us most of the day. He sensed something serious was happening and was getting 'stressy' as his mum calls it, and when he's 'stressy' he calms down best in a moving vehicle.

The plan is to do one last drive around to check no one has been missed before we cordon off all access routes to the village.

Dr Shah's phone rings. Someone is talking loud and fast.

'I see. Yes, yes, of course. She's my patient. I'll be there in twenty minutes.' He turns to Dad. 'It's Mrs Midgley. I need to get to Skeldale right away. You'll have to drive me.'

'Leave us here,' I say. 'We'll do the road blocks. Six roads, you said. Come on! Get the cones and the tape. We'll be fine – you can come back for us later.'

Dad swivels round in his seat. 'I'm not sure, Halo. We can't just leave you alone here.'

But the three of us are already piling out of the van.

'There's still plenty of time,' I say. 'Pick us up at the same place.'

Norman starts to wail and I take his hand. 'Come with us then, Norman. Here, you're going to help with the tape.'

He clasps the roll of red and white barrier tape. 'Blithering heck! Blithering heck! Blithering heck!' he shouts.

Pedro grabs the traffic cones and Silverlocks and I lift out the two 'Road Closed' signs that Dad borrowed from the council.

I bang the van door closed. 'Go! Go!' I shout to Dad, and they speed off down the road.

'The "Road Closed" signs should go at either end of Main Street,' I say.

'I'll do the library end,' says Pedro.

'I'll go to Moor Road,' says Silverlocks.

'Norman, we're doing the tape. Everyone meet up back here when you're finished.'

We stride downhill and see Dad's van speeding off into the distance. I help Norman tie the tape to fences and trees, wrapping it around several times to make sure it stays secure. Apparently, it's photoluminescent, which means it glows in car headlights. Norman runs backwards and forwards across the road, as if it's a game. I'm not sure he understands what it's really for.

We head up Hebden Hill where the road rises to Grimbalds reservoir and on towards Leeds. A magpie hops along the grass verge. It watches us as we attach the tape to a fence, slipping the other end through a gap in a dry-stone wall.

One for sorrow, says the rhyme in my head.

'Two more to roads to go,' I say.

We march along Main Street and Norman gets distracted by the gifts in the Hotchpotch.

'Come on,' I say. 'Stretch your legs and swing your arms and quick march!'

I walk alongside him. 'Left, right, left, right!' I chant.

Norman does the same. He's laughing and clapping.

'That's it, Norman. That's proper marching, well done.'

'Diddly-doo-dah!' he shouts back.

At the top of Kirkby Road, I look down at the river. There are patches of mist over the water and a deep, deep silence.

'What's going to happen, Norman?' I say. 'Will all this be here tomorrow?'

I think of the Chicxulub asteroid that wiped out the dinosaurs. The Tunguska meteor that flattened eighty million trees. The one in Chelyabinsk that injured a thousand people.

'Please don't let it destroy all this,' I whisper.

Norman shuffles around me and gently wipes away a tear.

'Thank you,' I say.

We attach the tapes across Kirkby Road and walk back. Dad's already there with the van, and on the other side Pedro and Silverlocks are waiting for us.

'That makes fifteen trips today,' says Dad. 'I'm shattered. Completely done in.'

'How is Mrs Midgley?' asks Silverlocks.

'She's been taken to hospital again,' he says. 'They think she'll be all right. Probably the stress of all this moving.'

'Have you been crying?' whispers Pedro.

'A bit,' I say.

He puts his arm around my shoulder. 'We'll be all right, Halo Moon. This time tomorrow, it'll be all over.'

TWO . . .

28

Halo

For a split second, I don't know where I am. I sit up and look around.

Skeldale library. The day of the meteor.

My heart revs up. I throw back the blanket, jump up and glance at my phone. Four seventeen. Still dark outside.

Silverlocks and Pedro are curled up under blankets. Carmela is fast asleep in the corner. I see Gran's white hair under her pink duvet.

But I don't see Norman. I scan along the lines of mattresses. I get up and tiptoe between the beds. There's Jade and Jessy and Ella. I pad around the library, carefully lifting corners of sheets and duvets when I can't see the faces. I don't see Norman anywhere.

'Silverlocks,' I whisper. I touch him gently. His eyes flicker open and I press a finger to my lips. 'Norman's gone.'

He sits up with wide eyes. He bounces to his feet and looks all around.

'Pedro.' I'm close to his ear and he gasps. 'Shh! Quiet! We can't find Norman.'

We're all out of bed, creeping around bookshelves, behind the librarian's desk, into the computer room and the children's section.

Then I remember. I wave to Pedro and Silverlocks and we huddle by the front door.

'I forgot his toy rabbit,' I whisper. 'His mum asked me to get it yesterday and I forgot. What if he's gone home to find it?'

'You should tell her,' says Pedro.

'I can't,' I say. 'I feel so bad. Let's just go and look for him. We'll probably be back before anyone wakes up.'

Pedro pauses. I can see he's not sure.

'What will happen if his mother wakes up and sees he is not here?' says Silverlocks.

'Then she'll call us and we can tell her what happened. Anyway, we'll have found him by then. Please, let's just go. We're wasting time.'

We take off towards the town hall, careering around corners, powering across Skeldale Market

Place and down the dark empty streets. The moon is gleaming down on us. We stop at the road that goes up to Thribbleston.

'It'll be quicker over the fields,' I say.

'What if he is walking on the road?' says Silverlocks.

'What if he's not going this way at all?' says Pedro.

'I'm hoping he's heading back home for his rabbit but I know he's never been anywhere on his own before. Let's spread out. Silverlocks, follow the road, Pedro in the middle of the field and me on the far side.'

It's hard trudging uphill especially when you can barely see in front of you. We step into the pools of light from our phones. We call to him.

'Norman! Norman!' we yell into the darkness.

I'm trying not to think that he could have lost his way, that he's heading in another direction and that in less than two hours a meteor is going to fall on Pockley Moor.

We're scrambling over walls between fields. There's no time to look for gates or stiles. We stumble and fall on hidden ridges and thick clumps of grass. The field is narrowing now, funnelling us back towards the road.

'He was here,' shouts Silverlocks. He's perched on the wall, waving a broken end of the luminescent tape.

'Keep following the road,' I yell. 'We need to move faster!'

We soon reach Metcalfe's farm. It belongs to Ella's grandad. We're running out of time but I know exactly what we need. I head straight for the barn and haul open the doors.

'What are you doing?' asks Pedro.

I shine my light inside.

'Grab a bike,' I say. 'We need to get back on the road.'

We run with the bikes across the field and haul them over the wall. Pedro clicks on the lights and we shoot through the dark to catch Silverlocks.

'Get on,' says Pedro. Silverlocks perches on the saddle as Pedro speeds off, balancing on the pedals.

We're all shouting now.

'Norman! Norman!'

We reach Thribbleston around five o'clock. We

take a left at the parish church and tear down Halley Road. Silverlocks and I race around the back of Norman's house. The key is on top of the mat.

'It's always *under* the mat,' I say. 'He must have been here.'

I unlock the door and charge upstairs to his room. The rabbit's not on the bedside table. I scan the carpet and peer under his bed. Scrabble through cupboards and drawers.

Silverlocks is searching downstairs. 'I cannot see anything,' he shouts up.

'He's been here already!' I yell. 'The rabbit's gone.'

Back out on the street, the stars are sparkling above.

'Silverlocks, head up Goosecroft Lane then search this end of Moor Road. I'll do the rest of Halley Road, up Kirkby and along Main Street. Pedro, you do Dr Shah's, Withers Road and Cold Edge Lane. Call if you find him. We'll meet up by the Craven Arms in ten minutes. No later.'

Past home, then up Kirkby Road to the edge of the park at the far end of the village. I shout for him. 'Norman! Norman!'

Past the 'Closed' sign in the Spar and the blinds pulled down in the library windows. Clambering over the wall and into the primary school now, shouting for him in the playground. I picture him at the top of the slide or rocking on the swings.

'Norman, it's Halo. Where are you?'

I run up the playing fields. My voice strains with shouting. But there's no one. The place is empty.

Almost at the end of the village, I turn up Hebden Hill. The sky's lightening and there's a thin fringe of orange on the horizon. Clouds are huddled behind the hills and even though a cool wind is blowing, Mr Gubbins's windmill stands motionless in his garden. A dreadful feeling creeps over me as I stride around the deserted streets and empty houses. Soon, a meteor is going to fall, and we're directly in its path.

'Norman! It's Halo! We're here, Norman! All your friends.'

'It's almost five-thirty,' says Pedro. 'They'll be waking up in Skeldale soon.'

'Right,' I say, 'one last try up Goosecroft Lane then we'll head up Moor Road. He has to be somewhere.'

29

Halo

We find a pink and grey furry ear lying further up Moor Road. Silverlocks spots it first.

'It must have fallen off,' he says. He picks it up. There are threads dangling from one end.

'Oh, no,' I say. 'He's heading for the moor.'

We power up the long strip of dark road. We're gritting our teeth, willing our limbs to move faster. We leave the bikes by the stile. They'll be no good on rough grass and bracken.

Scrambling over the stile and tearing up the path, we're soon stepping on to Pockley Moor, where the wind hits us like a wall and whips away our cries.

'Nor-man! Nor-man!'

We're searching the ridges and hollows and pathways, imagining him crouching in copses of trees or behind boulders and rocks.

'Nor-man!' we shout.

I race towards Wiccie's Circle in case he's found his way there. The shadowy stones stand in the flat ring of grass as they've done for centuries. Beyond them, in the pale light, are fields and hills and the deep blue sky stretching all around. We can't see Norman anywhere.

'Halo!' shouts Pedro. He grabs my hand. 'Let's get up on to High Crag. We might spot him from there.'

The slope is almost vertical in places. We clamber up, slipping on loose stones, grabbing tufts of wiry grass to steady ourselves.

'What's supposed to happen before a meteor falls?' shouts Pedro. The wind is so strong it's hard to hear each other.

I've watched the videos of the Chelyabinsk meteor loads of times.

'Nothing!' I scream. 'That's the trouble with them. There is no warning!'

Somewhere up there is a piece of space rock in the asteroid belt between Mars and Jupiter. It's been circling for four point six billion years. There's a disturbance, a knock, a collision and part of it breaks off, sending a fragment tumbling and spinning towards Earth. That's where it is now. On its way. Coming closer and closer as every second passes.

'Can't see him!' I shout. 'Let's head for the waterfall.'

Silverlocks's long legs carry him nimbly over the terrain. He's down the path passing the witchy tree before we're over the ridge.

As we wind down the stony path we see him below, pointing. Norman's there, next to the warning notice. 'DANGER. Slippery slope. Do not enter the water at any time.'

He's staring down at the river and in his hand is a velvet rabbit with one ear.

'I'll go,' I whisper to Pedro.

The noise of the river drowns every other sound. I tread carefully. I don't want to startle him. Keeping my distance, I squat on the path so he'll see me if he turns. Seconds pass, then Norman shuffles forward. He looks up, glances at me and smiles.

'Ha-lo!' he shouts. 'Bunny!'

'Wait for me, Norman,' I yell. 'We have to hold

hands. We're going to see the waterfall.'

Pedro and Silverlocks scramble down the path.

'What about getting back to Skeldale?' shouts Pedro.

'How?' I yell. 'It's nearly six! No time! We've got to hide.'

'Where?' says Silverlocks.

'There's only one place,' I say.

Pedro nods and leads the way.

The path narrows. We drop down amongst ferns and green mossy trunks. I take Norman's hand. He grabs my jacket in his other hand as we edge along, glancing down nervously at the steep drop.

'Let's put Bunny somewhere safe,' I say. 'In here. Look, we found his lost ear.'

He lets me tuck the toy into his pocket and zip it up.

'Now we have to march, Norman – do you remember how to do that? Nice long steps and there'll be a surprise at the end. Left, right, left, right!'

We keep glancing upwards. Knowing that it's on its way. Knowing that in half an hour a meteor will burst through the Earth's atmosphere and explode.

'Let's get moving,' I say. 'We'll pretend we're in a hurry because the shops are closing.'

Norman giggles and shuffles a little faster. Pedro moves to the front to take Norman's other hand to hurry him along.

Beside us the river churns. A dark, unstoppable force.

'Raining,' says Norman. I can hardly hear him now.

'It's the spray,' I shout. 'From the waterfall.'

I think of Dad. Imagine him strolling through the streets of Skeldale to the library, standing in the doorway with his hands in his pockets searching for us amongst the camp beds, mattresses and lilos. I should have called him. What if he's realised we're not there and he's coming after us? What if he's out here when the meteor strikes?

My heart revs up again. I glance at my phone. No signal.

'Come on, Norman. As quickly as you can.'

We step carefully. We're climbing up the rocks next to the waterfall. We show him where to place his feet, which rocks to hold on to. When he slips, we catch him. When his face is scrunched up against the spray, we hold his hands and lead him on.

The branches at the entrance are exactly as we left them.

'One big push, Norman,' I say. He heaves himself up the side of the boulder and we're in front of the cave. It's almost level with the top of the waterfall.

Silverlocks takes off his backpack, gently drops it on to the cave floor, then slips through the gap into the dark cavern. He turns to face us, taking out his phone.

'Pass yours,' he says to Pedro.

Silverlocks swipes both phones and the lights come on. He places them near the entrance.

Norman peers in.

'It is safe in here,' says Silverlocks. 'Like a beautiful stone house. Come inside and bring your rabbit.'

Norman hesitates. I can see his brow crumpling and his mouth quivering, as if he's going to cry.

'We're going to pretend this is our house,' I say.

'We're all going to go through this door and inside we can have a story.' I hold his hand. 'Let's shout,' I say. 'Let's all shout, "Summa's 'ere!"'

The three of us yell at the tops of our voices. Norman smiles and edges closer.

'Put your leg here and your hand there,' I say.

He's on top of the rock now, ready to slip through.

'A little more. Just a bit further. Silverlocks will make sure you don't fall.'

We ease Norman sideways through the gap. He tips, slides, then he's on the cave floor, gazing at the stalactites.

I glance at my phone. One bar is lit.

'I'm calling Dad,' I say.

The phone rings once. Dad's screaming.

'Where the hell are you? I've been trying to get you for ages!'

'We're on the moor. I forgot to get Norman's rabbit from his house and he went off to find it some time during the night. When I realised we all came to the village to look for him. He's here and we're OK. All of us. We're hiding in a cave.'

I hear Mum crying.

'Let me speak to her,' I hear her say, and there's a scrabbling sound as she takes Dad's phone. 'What are you doing, Halo? We're worried sick.'

'We're safe, Mum. We're in a cave by Ingilby Foss. The thing is, if we set off now . . . well, it's best if we stay here, until . . . we'll just stay here. We'll be OK.'

'Stay exactly where you are. Dad's coming to get you.'

'No! Don't let him! There's no time. It's too dangerous. No one is to move. We'll be safe here. I promise you we'll be OK. Just wait till it's all over.'

The signal dies and I try to call back.

'Come on, Halo,' says Pedro.

We glance at the sky one more time, then climb through.

30

Silverlocks

I sit on the cave floor, blinking, waiting for my eyes to get used to the darkness. It is cold in here and water is dripping through cracks in the rocks. I find a dry place for Norman and we sit and listen to the waterfall, like a thousand hands clapping.

'You seen this?' says Pedro.

He is at the back of the cave, shining his phone light into a gap between the broken stones.

'Those must have fallen recently,' says Halo. 'I've never seen this space before.'

'Need to get this lot out of the way,' says Pedro. He starts to move bits of rock.

'Why?' asks Halo.

'In case we need another exit.' Pedro pulls at the loose stones and we help to pile them by the side of the chamber.

'Careful, everyone!' he yells.

A larger rock tumbles and rolls. Norman shouts

and covers his ears.

'I'm going to take a look,' says Pedro, and he disappears through the gap.

'What's in there?' shouts Halo.

'You'll never believe it.' His voice sounds like it is coming from far away. 'Come and see.'

'You go,' I say to Halo. 'I will wait here with Norman.'

She moves towards the gap but Norman stands up. He wants to go too.

'Come on, then,' says Halo. 'We'll all go.'

Halo takes Norman's hand and I hold his other hand to keep him steady.

I say, 'Put your feet on the flat rocks. Take little steps.'

Water drips, splashing our faces. Another little step and another. I shine the light on to Norman's feet and the broken rock and puddles of water.

'Keep going,' I say. 'Step on the next rock. And the next. And the next.'

Pedro holds out a hand and pulls Norman along. Then he is through and on the other side and his eyes are shining.

'Bet you've never done that before,' says Pedro.

'Blithering heck! Blithering heck! Blithering heck!' shouts Norman. I think he feels afraid.

There is no way out to the moor on this side, but it is a bigger space and there is blue sky through a crack in the rock. We climb up and look out at the silver grass and the clouds and the green hills.

'We're above the waterfall,' says Halo. 'Level with the moor. And it all looks so peaceful out there.'

We sit quietly in our new place. I think of the rock around us, hoping it will be strong enough to protect us. I imagine the meteor, again and again, and each time the same terrible thing happens.

'We should say something,' says Halo. 'You know, just in case.'

We have been silent for so long, her voice frightens us.

'Like what?' says Pedro.

'I dunno. Like if we survive this I'll take you all to Nando's for sunset burgers. Or, I'm absolutely terrified right now.'

I reach for her hand and Norman comes closer and wraps his arms around her.

'Me, too,' says Pedro. 'But when we survive this,

I'm going to be as brave as my dad so I can help my mum and my sister.'

I smile.

'I will thank everyone for believing us, most of all, Dr Shah,' I say. 'I will apologise to my parents for deceiving them but I will say that I have learned more from coming to Yorkshire than I ever would from summer school and I have friends that will be my friends for ever.'

'Friends-friends, friends-friends,' says Norman.

And we sit there, all of us, holding on to each other, telling ourselves that we will be all right, we will walk away from this and we will live another day.

ONE . . .

31

Halo

There is no warning.

It appears out of nowhere. A giant streak shooting through the sky. It looks like an exploding plane, or a missile, but it is much faster and much, much brighter. We watch it with scrunched-up eyes through the gap in the rock, powering towards us, bulging and fire-hot at its head, leaving a thick, billowing trail behind. It approaches silently at first, absolute silence that seems to go on for ever, then it swells into a huge glowing ball as bright as the sun. The glare is blinding. The ball hurtles over us and moments later, the sound waves hit us and we hear it explode. Guy Fawkes night times a billion. Blasts and booms as loud as bombs. We press our hands to our ears, burying our heads, believing the world is ending.

The world is ending and we're all going to end with it.

The bangs and rumbles go on for minutes. Through the gap I see the rippling white vapour trail hanging in the sky.

Pedro stretches a hand towards me. 'We're here,' he whispers. 'We're all still here.'

We get to our feet. Breathing fast. Trembling all over. Edging to the gap so we can look out.

No heather. No bracken. No wispy yellow grass. No paths to High Crag or Wiccie's Circle. Just rocks and stones and red earth everywhere. Pockley Moor has gone.

There's a horrible creaking sound and a gigantic crash outside.

'What was that?' I shout.

'Don't know!' yells Pedro. 'Rocks falling. Get out of here, now!'

We jump up and push through the gap. We hurry Norman as best we can. He's crying and wailing, seized by panic.

Squeezing out through the entrance, Silverlocks struggles with his backpack.

'I'll help you,' I yell. 'Keep the Device safe!'

The sky is a weird shade of brown and a fine dust is falling. We smell it, taste it, feel it on our faces. Over on the bank, every tree is leaning like a giant hand reached out and pushed them over. There's a loud groan then a tremendous *crack!* One of them topples behind us, smashing over the rocks, sending showers of splinters into the air. Pine needles scatter everywhere.

'Move!' I yell.

We clamber down the side of the waterfall. We're scrambling over rocks and wood that weren't here before. There's no way up to the bank again and we can't climb beyond the cave. The only way is towards the river. Another tree shivers and starts to tip. Rocks and soil tumble down the slope. It seems like the whole bank is sliding, carrying the trees with it.

'Faster!'

'There's nowhere to go,' shouts Pedro.

'In the river!' I scream. 'Everyone! Get in!'

We scramble over the rocks by the water, keeping close together, guiding Norman and steadying each other. Silverlocks drags a fallen branch to the water's edge.

We stand there looking at each other, all of us realising that this is the only possible way to get out of here.

'Hold on and do not let go!' Silverlocks shouts.

The cold takes our breath away. We can hardly bear to move. In minutes, our fingers, arms and legs are numb. Above, dust from the moorland darkens the sky, blotting out the sunlight. Ahead, the dark river rolls along in great swirling pools.

'When we're near the village, get out on the bank!' I yell. My jaw is clenched and I'm already shivering.

Pedro pushes us into the main flow. He's behind Norman, holding on to him as the river carries us along. It flows fast and strong. We're trying to steer ourselves away from rocks but in the shallower water our feet drag and crash into hidden boulders. Norman's eyes are tightly closed as he hugs the log with all his strength. The frothing brown mass carries us, squeezing between pillars of rock, whilst behind, dark clouds hang over Pockley Moor.

It's deeper now. The current is so strong there's no point trying to fight it. We shoot over another, smaller rapid. The log spins and in an instant Silverlocks loses his grip, crashes into me and suddenly we're both under the water. The force of the falls pushes us deeper, swirling us upside down.

Which way is up? Where is the light? I swim anyway, crashing my legs into rocks as I kick and emerge and gasp, heaving in lungfuls of air.

I can't see Silverlocks. I don't even know if he can swim. I imagine the weight of the Portendo Device in the backpack dragging him down.

I dive but it's impossible to see anything in the churning darkness. I flail about, surge forward, turn and twist trying to find him. I'm not strong enough to swim against the current and I let the water take me to the surface again. Then I spot him ahead of me. The top of his head, a hand holding on, his mouth drawing in air, and a moment later he's dragged under again. I fight the flow to get to him, kicking and heaving myself forward. Out of the corner of my eye I see Pedro and Norman way ahead, drifting further and further downstream.

'Hold on!' I yell. 'Just hold on!'

I crash into the boulders behind Silverlocks. He's slipped underneath now with one hand still gripping a small lip of rock above water level. I find a handhold and haul myself out. From the top of the rocks, I lean over, grab Silverlocks's hand and pull. I have him for a few seconds then he slips and he's under again. I'm shivering with cold and shaking with fear.

'Silverlocks!' I yell. 'Sil-ver-locks!'

He bobs to the surface downstream, floating now rather than swimming. I charge along the bank. The surface is flatter here and I'm ahead of him again. I'm straddling two boulders, watching him approaching. My hands hover at water level waiting for him to pass, then I grab hold of his arm and try to haul him out.

'I will not let you go!' I yell. I keep pulling, twisting him around, grasping him under his arms. 'Help me, Silverlocks! Push with your feet!'

He does nothing. He seems limp and lifeless. I force myself to try again, mustering all the energy I have. I give one gigantic roar and drag him upwards. He's balancing sideways on the edge now. I grab his legs, one at a time, roll him away from the water and onto the rocks. His eyes are shut and I lean in closer, waiting to feel his breath.

'Come on! Come on, Silverlocks! Breathe!'

Puffs of cool air on my cheek.

He is alive.

I slip the backpack from his shoulders, take him in my arms, enclose him with my whole body trying to warm him. And all the time I'm whispering, 'You're all right. You're safe now. You're safe.'

The river is wider here, and darker. Pedro and Norman have gone.

'Can you stand?' I say.

'I do not know,' he breathes.

I bend, pull him up so he's sitting, haul him to standing. The Device is in the backpack strapped to my front and we start walking. Slowly.

We manage fifty steps then have to stop. We're both exhausted from cold and fear.

Silverlocks' eyes are closed.

'Are you all right?' I whisper.

He's barely able to nod. Part of his face is red and small patches of skin are beginning to peel.

'What colour is my face?' I say.

'Pink,' he whispers, 'around your eyes, like the sun has burned it.'

'It's the heat from the meteor,' I say.

I dig into my jeans for my phone, try to switch it

on but water drips from inside and the screen is blank.

I put my arm around him again, picturing marathon runners and mountain climbers, cyclists on the Tour de France. They keep going. They find strength from somewhere to battle on.

Further along the bank I start to recognise the fields. We're at the back of Hargreaves' Farm. I lower Silverlocks on to the grass and scan the river for Pedro and Norman, trying not to think what may have happened to them.

I lay the backpack beside him.

'D'you think the Device will still work?' I say.

'I do not know,' he whispers.

'Can you walk any further?'

'You go,' he says.

'But I don't want to leave you.'

'Please,' he says. 'I will rest. When you come back with Pedro and with Norman, I will be feeling better.'

'I'll find them,' I say. 'I'll bring them back. I promise.'

32

Halo

The vapour trail from the meteor hangs across the sky like a thick white band. Sirens screech in the distance. I wonder what's happened to the village and if everyone's safe in Skeldale.

The river flows fast and thick and muddy brown. I scramble over the fence and push through hawthorn trees on to the bank.

'Pedro! Norman!' I shout.

I search the bushes, scan the trees on the far bank across the river. Peer into the deep, dark rushing water. I'm running now, between rocks, over flat stones, much too close to the edge. Climbing down steep banks where the water tumbles over mini waterfalls.

'Pedro! Norman!'

There are parts too dangerous to walk along and I climb back up to follow the fields.

It's my fault, I keep thinking. *It's my fault they*

came up here.

Then a voice. A movement under the trees.

'Ha-lo! Ha-lo! Ha-lo!'

'Pedro! Norman!' I yell.

I scramble down the steep slope, slipping on stones and soil.

'Where are you?'

'Here.' It's Pedro's voice.

I'm sliding now, hanging on to clumps of grass, digging my heels into the earth.

He's lying there amongst the ferns. I kneel and throw my arms around him.

'I thought you'd gone! I thought the river had taken you!'

'Halo,' he says. He closes his eyes and breathes deeply. 'Silverlocks? Where is he?'

'On the bank further up. Too tired to walk. He went under. Got stuck. I thought I'd lost him.' Tears start to spill.

Pedro's jeans are ripped and blood is seeping from his leg.

'Can you walk?'

'Don't know. Haven't tried.'

'Is your phone working?'

He shakes his head.

'Lost it. In the river. Go and find Norman. He hasn't stopped calling for you.'

'Ha-lo. Ha-lo! Ha-lo!'

I make my way down the bank. I can see him now, sitting on a rock close to the edge of the water, searching for me, his shoulders shuddering.

'Ha-lo. Ha-lo! Ha-lo!'

I tread softly, trying not to startle him.

'I'm here,' I say, softly. 'Halo is here now.'

Norman turns. He gets up. He wraps his arms around me.

'We are all OK,' I say, holding him close. 'Halo and Silverlocks and Pedro and Norman are all OK. You've been so brave.'

He clutches my hand and wipes his tears and we pull Pedro to his feet and help him up the bank to the fields to where Silverlocks is waiting.

Smoke drifts up from the village. The whole shape of it seems to have changed. Roofs have gone. Chimneys are missing. We move as fast as we can through fields to the top of Kirkby Road. I know we shouldn't be here. I know it's dangerous.

'Come on! We need to find a phone,' I say. 'Need to let them know we're OK.'

There's dust everywhere. Roofs and green lawns are covered in the fine, brown powder. It's still falling. I blink it from my eyes and rub it from my face. We walk through the village trying to take it all in. Pedro still limping. Silverlocks shivering and coughing.

We turn on to Main Street. Tiles have tumbled and smashed. The glass has been blown out of windows. Some have disappeared completely, punched inside by the blast. Chimneys have collapsed and fallen to the ground, scattering bricks across the road.

The Spar, sheltered by a high wall, seems to have avoided the worst of the sonic boom. Only a few packs of toilet rolls have been knocked down from a display in the window.

And then the library. I start to run. I hear Silverlocks's and Pedro's footsteps behind me. What we see is such a shock that we stop dead in the road and stare.

One side of the building has been torn away and part of the roof has gone. A thick metal girder that was holding everything up stretches bare across the sky. One wall is just a pile of bricks and rubble. Books, bookshelves and broken glass are strewn across the car park.

I slump down with my head in my hands.

'What's Mrs Moira Hattersley going to say?'

We could have guessed that the buildings nearest the moor would be worse. Windows blown in with such force that the frames went with them. Most of the roof has gone from the Craven Arms and the insides of Mrs Clegg's newsagents are strewn across the pavement. In a more sheltered corner, the sign on Siddle's Chip Shop droops sideways from the wall.

Norman stands in the road, trying to understand what's happened.

Past the church now. Dark spaces loom where the windows once were. Splinters of stained glass lie scattered between gravestones. Then Halley Road. My road. My home for twelve years. We stride down the middle looking back at our footprints in the dust.

Only a few tiles gone from the Howeths' roof

and Barry Ackroyd's bungalow, but all of the Fitchetts' front windows have been blown in. It's the same for Pedro's, and his front door is hanging on one hinge.

He goes over.

'Not so bad inside,' he says. 'And at least we still have a roof.'

Norman's staring at his own house, his eyes full of tears.

'It was the meteor,' I explain. 'It broke everything. But we're going to fix it. Exactly like it was before.'

He takes the little rabbit from deep in his pocket. He presses it to his face and strokes its velvet ear.

'Come on,' I say. 'Let's see what it's like in my house.'

The key is still under the flowerpot. I turn it, push the door and step into the kitchen. Cupboard doors have swung open. Plates have fallen and broken. Even those still on the shelves have cracked. Packets of pasta and cans are strewn over the table and floor. Most of the conservatory windows have fallen through, but my telescope stands in the corner, untouched.

We creep through the house as if we're expecting someone. The cause of all this chaos. Books fallen from bookshelves. The carpets littered with glass.

Pedro goes over to the hall table and picks up the phone receiver.

'It's working,' he says.

I call Mum and she cries and cries. Dad can hardly speak.

'We're safe,' I say. 'All of us. Norman, Pedro. Silverlocks. We're all OK.'

'And Norman? What about Norman?' shouts Mrs Fitchett.

'He's here,' I say. 'He's with us here and he's fine.'

Then Dad's voice again. 'Halo. Thank God you're all right. Where are you?'

'Home,' I say. 'It's a mess. I mean, the whole village is a mess. But we're all OK.'

'Is it safe in there?' says Mum.

'Stay where you are,' shouts Dad. 'We're coming to get you.'

We suddenly realise how thirsty we are. There's

orange juice in the fridge and we gulp it down straight from the carton. I dig out Dad's biscuit tin. What we don't manage to eat, we stuff in our pockets. It seems pointless to lock the door before we leave, but I do it anyway.

And it's only when I'm in the van rumbling back along Skeldale Road, warm and safe in Mum's arms, that I cry.

Sometime later, in Skeldale library, Dr Shah is checking our cuts and grazes and the burns on our faces. My hands are still trembling and my head is buzzing.

'You've been extremely brave,' says the doctor. 'And you've all been very lucky.'

Mum and Dad are here with Rose and Carmela. I already saw Gran in the town hall. We hugged for ages and wiped away each other's tears.

'Have you called your parents?' Mum asks Silverlocks, softly.

'Not yet,' he says.

'Call them now.' She passes her phone. 'It'll be on all the news channels. They'll be worried sick.'

Silverlocks takes the phone and looks to the floor.

'I must explain,' he says.

'I'll tell them, if you like,' I say.

'That is very kind, Halo, but it is me who has deceived everyone.'

'What d'you mean?' says Mum.

Silverlocks glances at Dr Shah.

'My parents are not here in England. They live in Addis Ababa. They think I am at summer school in Oxford.'

'Oh, my goodness,' says Mum. 'I thought they knew and they were going to come and collect you soon.'

'So they've no idea that you're here?' says Rose.

'I had to come here myself with the Device or no one would have believed the prediction,' says Silverlocks. 'If I had told my parents they would not have let me come at all.'

Dr Shah nods. 'It was the right decision and you have only our gratitude and our praise.'

Rose wraps her arms around him and Mum comes to hug him too. 'You must call them, but don't feel ashamed. You're an amazing young man. They'll be so proud of you,' she says.

'Come with me,' says Dad. 'I'll find a quiet place.'

They set up a video conference in the computer room of the library. We overhear snippets of conversation through the door. Silverlocks tells them what has happened then Dad explains why Silverlocks felt he had to lie about being at summer school when he was coming to save our village.

'He's an absolute hero,' says Dad. 'He lost most of his money in London so he walked *two hundred* miles to get here. He's saved many, many lives.'

Dad comes out and we leave Silverlocks alone to talk with his mum and dad. And then I realise that he'll be gone soon, back to Ethiopia, and we may never see him again.

Jade rushes in.

'Oh my god, Halo!' She runs to me and hugs me tight. 'What happened to your face?'

'Radiation burn from the meteorite,' I say.

'Really? We were so panicked when we couldn't find you. They said you were on the moor when it came down.'

'We went to find Norman.'

'Oh my god! You're so brave.' She takes my hand and we sit there as other villagers come in to thank us.

'Flipping celebrity now, aren't you?' says Jade. 'You'll be in the *Skeldale Gazette*. *Yorkshire Times*, probably.' She looks down suddenly, scrunches up her eyes. 'I was terrified, Halo. We all were. Thought that was it, you know. Thought you'd all gone for ever.'

I smile and we hug.

'Got some news . . .' she says. 'Best news ever. I'm not going to that Nottingham school any more.'

'Oh! That's great!' I say.

'I promised Mum and Dad I'll stop messing about and get serious with my studying. Dead weird that device knew about it though. What's going to happen to it now?'

'Dunno. He'll probably take it back.'

'Bit of a shame, though, isn't it? I mean, think what you could do with it. You could become a superhero with a thing like that.'

I laugh. 'Yeah, you probably could.'

33

Silverlocks

The sky is full of dust and smoke. The army has arrived and no one can return to the village until every building has been checked and made safe. There are men in uniforms standing on the roads and in fields to stop anyone going back. At the edge of my mind are visions of what would have happened if I had not found the Device, if I had not come to England to warn everyone. I try to push those thoughts away.

It is still early in the morning but many film crews and news reporters are arriving in Skeldale. The meteor is world-wide news. I think of Ma and Da watching it back home with no idea that I was so close when it fell. Television vans with big satellite dishes are blocking the streets and there are two helicopters flying over the moor.

There is not enough space for everyone in the town hall, so a big man in army uniform stands on a platform in the town square.

'You will be relieved to hear,' he says through a microphone, 'that for most houses the main damage is to the windows, which have been blown in. Some houses have fallen chimneys, broken roof slates, but some properties do have major damage and may have to be rebuilt. Tomorrow morning, we will be delivering temporary accommodation in the form of static caravans on the fields next to the village for those who cannot return to their homes immediately.'

'Well, that's very nice,' says the chip shop lady. 'If we're in a caravan, it'll be like being on holiday. Mind you, it's going to take a while to get my fish and chip shop up and running again.'

Later, we pass Mrs Clegg in the Copper Kettle tea shop. She is talking to ITV News. Then we see Mr Ackroyd sitting on a park bench telling his story to reporters from CNN.

One of the reporters sees us and waves.

'Come on,' says Halo, and we run.

We do not want to talk yet. We are not ready. We need to be somewhere quiet and calm. Halo takes us through alleyways and narrow streets into the church where it is still and cool and silent. We climb the winding steps, holding on to the rail and the cold stone wall, and out into the light again. We are in a tiny space looking out over Skeldale and Thribbleston and the moor.

'Were we really in a cave when a meteor fell?' says Halo.

'Running like crazy from a landslide and falling trees,' says Pedro.

'Almost drowning in a freezing river.'

Halo turns to me. She looks deep into my eyes. 'You came here from Ethiopia. You walked for days and days. You saved a whole village. How can we ever thank you?'

'You would have done the same,' I say.

Halo shakes her head. 'I don't think I could ever be that brave.'

I turn away. I watch the busy people in the streets below.

Pedro stares into the distance. 'I need to use the Device,' he says.

Halo glances at me, then back at Pedro.

'Are you sure?' she asks him.

Pedro nods.

'Did you tell Silverlocks . . . you know . . . about your dad?' she whispers.

Pedro looks to the floor. 'No,' he says.

We sit down on the grey stones of the tower. I slip off my bag and lift out the ancient device with its three gleaming discs and three black pointers and place it on the ground. Pedro breathes in and breathes out. He stares at it for a while.

'D'you think it can tell me?' he says.

I do not know what has happened to his father but I see pain in his eyes, and sadness.

'I am not sure,' I whisper.

Halo wraps her arms around him and holds him tight. We watch his fingers tremble as they touch the metal. His eyes flicker and close as if he cannot bear to look. The pointer turns. Halo covers her face.

I read out the symbols and their meaning, then Pedro stands and whispers, 'Thank you,' before disappearing through the door and down the stairs.

34

Silverlocks

'Da!' I shout.

I race alongside the taxi until it stops outside Skeldale town hall. It is the day after the meteor and Da has travelled through the night to get here. He is wearing a smart suit and tie and has a serious look on his face. He pays the driver, opens the door and steps out.

'Ageze,' he says in his deep, soft voice. His eyes shine and a smile spreads across his face.

'Da!'

He wraps his arms around me. I cry. Many, many tears.

'I am sorry,' I say over and over. 'Please do not be angry. I am so sorry that I did not tell you the truth.'

'All that matters is that you are safe and well,' he says. He shakes his head. 'And how brave you have been, my son. I want to hear the story from the beginning to the end.'

Someone rushes up to us with a camera. Another news reporter. Then another arrives and another, shouting questions and pushing their microphones towards us.

'Over here!' It is Halo's father, waving for us to follow him. Da grabs my hand and we rush along the streets.

'In here. It'll be quieter.' Halo's father opens the library door. The reporters want to push their way in. 'Have some respect,' he says to them. 'This is the only home we have right now.'

Families are living here, like refugees, each with their own little space on the floor, alongside the bookshelves. They have nowhere else to go until the caravans arrive and their homes are repaired. It is a time for sorrow, but I do not see any sad faces.

Halo is here. And Pedro. Halo's father guides us to the computer room, where Halo's mother, Dr Shah and Rose are waiting. There is tea and coffee and fresh buns from the bakery and we all sit down to tell our story.

'It began at Grandma's house,' I say to Da.

I tell them about finding the Device near the church and discovering how to use it. Then the water spout and the factory fire and the terrible prediction of death. Of cancelling the summer school, losing my money and my long, long walk from London. Of the kindness of the people of Thribbleston and Halo's telescope and the stars and her prediction of the meteor. Pedro's strength and daring.

And all the time Da is watching me, not blinking once. When I have finished he stands up, reaches out to me and lifts me into his arms. Halo and Pedro jump up and come to hug us and we stay like that until all the words have been spoken and tears have been cried and we are smiling again.

Then I lift the Portendo Device on to the table.

Da leans closer. I watch his engineering mind trying to figure out how it works.

'What is powering it?' he asks.

'A key and some cogs,' says Halo.

He rests one hand on the base and the Device makes a whirring sound. He rubs his forehead. 'And it predicts?' he says. 'Predicts?'

'Not everything can be explained by science,' says Halo. 'You should try it.'

'Yes, Da,' I say. 'It may surprise you.'

I show him where to place his fingers.

'Open your mind,' I say, and we giggle.

Da sits quietly for a while. 'I think I would prefer not to interfere with things I do not understand. You have realised, I am sure, that if this Device is truly able to make predictions and was taken by someone who wanted to harm others, this would be a terrible thing. I believe it must go back to where you found it and its magic must be buried with it.'

'The Portendo Device is very powerful, Da, but all of the things it has predicted have helped, not harmed people.'

'I would like to think that is because *you* were using it, my son.' He takes me in his arms and hugs me.

'I have not thought about it that way, Da,' I say. 'Maybe you are right.'

35

Halo

Early the next morning, outside Skeldale library, we wait with them for the taxi. The knot in my stomach grows tighter. A blunt, hard feeling of how much I don't want this summer to end and one of the best friends I've ever had, to leave. I blot the tears from my cheeks. I hate crying.

'Weekly Skype call. Mondays. Six o'clock,' I say. I hug him again.

Silverlocks takes our hands in his. 'I solemnly promise that I will see you both soon, either in England, or Ethiopia.'

'I promise, too,' I whisper.

'Count me in,' says Pedro.

Dr Tadesse thanks everyone for looking after his son and Silverlocks hugs Mum and Dad and Gran and Rose. Then he hugs Pedro and me one last time, and climbs into the taxi.

'Look at the sky every night,' I call. 'We'll

see the same stars, won't we?'

'Yes, Halo Moon, we will always see the same stars.'

The door closes and the car moves away and our Ethiopian boy with silver in his hair and a smile like sunshine, the boy who walked two hundred miles to save us, waves goodbye.

Epilogue

Buried deep in the sandy soil under an ancient acacia tree in Ethiopia, lies an object of great beauty and power. It is wrapped in soft cloth and locked inside a metal case and only me, this one boy on the planet, knows where it is. Maybe, sometime in the future, it will be lifted from the earth once more and used to do good in the world. Until then, its location remains an absolute secret.

* * *

It's late December now. There's frost on the hedges and tyre tracks pressed into a thick layer of snow. In the bedroom in the house that's diagonally opposite mine there's someone new. His face is thin, his hair is short and he's standing at the window, laughing. And his smile is wide and lovely, just like Pedro's.

Author's Note

Dates and times are important in this story. The setting is both England and Ethiopia where the calendar and clock times are quite different. For purely practical reasons and to avoid my own befuddlement and that of the readers, standard time and the Gregorian calendar have been used throughout. By way of explanation, in England, times and dates are based on Greenwich Mean Time and the twelve-month Gregorian calendar. The Ethiopian calendar, rooted in the country's history and both the Coptic and Ethiopian Orthodox Tewahido churches, divides one year into thirteen months and is 7–8 years behind the Gregorian calendar. So, the thirteenth of August 2018 in the UK is the seventh of December 2010 in Ethiopia. As for telling the time, almost all Ethiopians use a twelve-hour clock when the start of the day is dawn (one o'clock) and the end of the day is dusk (twelve o'clock) with the next twelve-hour cycle from dusk to dawn.

Acknowledgements

My heartfelt thanks to:

Emmanuel, Birhan and family for your warm
welcome and insights into life in Ethiopia.

Hannah for kindly sharing your experiences
of Addis Ababa.

Richard N. for putting me in touch.

Dr Phil Sutton, Department of Physics,
Loughborough University, for an enlightening tour
of the observatory and stellar advice on stargazing.

Dr Ralph Lee, Teaching Associate in World
Christianities, Faculty of Divinity,
Cambridge University, for your enthusiasm,

expertise and guidance on Ethiopia and for
providing translations in the ancient language
of Ge'ez.

Louise Wilkinson, Head of Information and
Learning, Child Brain Injury Trust, who so kindly
gave information and advice on acquired brain
injury (ABI).
https://childbraininjurytrust.org.uk/

Professor Derick Wade, for his specialist advice
also on acquired brain injury (ABI).